MW01178737

Chantecler

A Story of Love

Victor Thomas Salupo

*To Marv & Joyce —
With Love!
Victor Salupo
1/7/2000*

**The
New Dawn Press**

The New Dawn Press
1375 East 40th Street
Cleveland, Ohio 44103

THE NEW DAWN PRESS and Colophon are registered trademarks
of The New Dawn Press

Interior Design: Sans Serif Inc.
Cover Design: Joseph Shirey
Cover Illustration: Sol Ehrlich

Manufactured in the United States of America

Publisher's Cataloging-in-Publication
(Provided by Quality Books, Inc.)
Salupo, Victor.
　　Chantecler : a story of love / Victor Thomas
Salupo. — 1st ed.
　　　p.　cm.
　　　Includes index.
　　　LCCN: 99-93329
　　　ISBN: 0-9672913-0-5

　　1. Roosters—Fiction.　2. Pheasants—Fiction.
3. Courtship of animals—Fiction.　4. Duty—Fiction.　I. Title

PS3569.A462325C43　1999　　　　　　813'.54
　　　　　　　　　　　　　　　　　　QBI99-910

For my partner and best friend in life,

Laura Greene,

Whom I admire, respect and love.

And

The many other kind and generous people

I have been blessed to have in my life.

Thank you with all my heart!

Contents

∽

Contents

The strongest and sweetest
songs yet remain to be sung.

Walt Whitman

The great tragedy of life is not that men
perish, but that they cease to love.

W. Somerset Maughn

There is not a woman in the world
the possession of whom is as
precious as that of the truths
which she reveals to us by
causing us to suffer.

Marcel Proust

Whoever really loves you will make you cry.

Anonymous Spanish Proverb

Where there is great love,
there are always miracles.

Willa Cather

I

———

The Dawning

*I*t was still night. Chantecler awoke with a start, terrified that he had overslept and that dawn had risen without him. He pulled himself together quickly and hurriedly made his way to a favorite spot beyond the barnyard. Although it was completely dark, some extra sensory perception allowed him to be sure-footed. But the exertion of hurrying left him short of breath.

Without pausing, he began to peck and push until he had cleared his spot of any stray weeds and stones. He then set his two feet firmly, north by northwest, readjusted his balance, and took a deep breath.

In his mind's eye he visualized the sounds that would be forthcoming. This was the moment that was most frightening to him because it raised the question of whether the reality of his sound would measure up to his vision of it.

Replanting his feet firmly again, he let go with his first sound. It was feeble and disappointing. His confidence was a little shaken. With greater determination, he tried again. This time the sound came forth more clear. Quickly, he tried again and it was stronger. His confidence began to grow. He took another deep breath, his chest expanded and he felt the blood rush to his head. And then, like a trumpet, a bold clarion call emerged that traveled the entire span of the valley.

Without pause now, he repeated the process, exerting every muscle in his body until the tension became excruciating. He continued in this precise way until his call was so bold, so clarion, the sun peeked out over a cloud. Emboldened by the sight of the sun, he increased his efforts, first steadily, then almost frantically. He pushed, he pulled, he stretched, he dug, demanding the sun to rise. The sun hesitated for a second causing Chantecler to sing a variation of his tune. It was so sensual and sweet and seductive the sun shone a little brighter.

Completely encouraged, Chantecler sang variation after variation, one more beautiful than the other. The sun, enchanted by his abandon and unabashed affection, now shone brilliantly, lighting up the mountaintop, cresting the flowers and the field with warmth and drenching the valley with such illumination that the night fled in haste.

Chantecler continued working passionately, his legs growing weak, and with his heart pounding wildly, his breath coming in short sharp blasts, he exploded with ecstasy. His head whirled out of control with dizziness and everything blurred and he fell to the ground in a faint.

As he gradually revived, he raised his head slightly and saw life stirring all around him once again. Slowly, the strength that comes with victory began to return to his body. He lay still and viewed the magnificent accomplishment he had wrought, and with great pride, basked in its glory.

II

~

King of the Barnyard

In the distance he could hear the chug, chug of the ancient automobile that belonged to the old farmer and his wife who were extremely poor. They had settled on this small patch of land many years ago, and more from necessity than conviction, had become vegetarians. Since their whole existence was meager they had few friends, and when the need for human contact became overwhelming, they visited an old couple some distance away. They had risen at daybreak so they could get an early start and now they were gone.

When they were out of sight, the Scarecrow, a ragged bag of straw stuffed into an old floursack-shirt and cover-alls worn from years of hard work, unhooked himself from the post, and once on the ground, wobbled his way toward the barnyard.

Not only did he look pathetic, thought Chantecler, but he knew the Scarecrow to be deeply unhappy. Even though he had form and substance, no one accepted him as real. He was simply looked upon as something to be used. And if that weren't bad enough, he was pecked at, sat on, and eaten. To add insult to injury, he was also ignored. I must be especially kind to him, Chantecler thought, and treat him seriously, for without his self respect and dignity, he will surely wither and blow away.

The valley was now drenched in warmth and the mountain sat majestically crested in a halo. The flowers gleamed with gold-dust and the barnyard sparkled, awash with the freshness of the dew.

Chantecler arose, fully recovered from his arduous task. He swelled with pride as he looked out over the field and into the barnyard. Patou, the dog, his dear old friend, was shaking free the last remnants of sleep. Later, under the shade of the tree, Chantecler would discuss the weightier aspects of life with him, as they did frequently. And even though they disagreed at times, it was always with special regard for each other.

Off to the side, Chantecler heard the high-pitched voice of Madam Guinea Hen. She was gathering the young chicks into a group near the water trough. She was an old dowager and the arbiter of the social set. And although Chantecler opposed her fashion shows, frivolous cocktail parties, and in general, her snobbishness, he tried—though with great difficulty—to be tolerant. He respected her age and the fact that she taught the young chicks lessons of history.

By ones and twos the hens jumped from their perches onto the ground where they scratched and picked bits of food. He made a mental note to remind them of the danger of pecking too near the road, which had recently become more traveled.

A commotion among the turkeys caught his attention and made him hasten his approach to the barnyard. But by the time he arrived and jumped to the stone wall bounding the area, the cluck and the clatter was in full squall.

"Here! Here!," he said. "The day has hardly begun and there is fighting! This should be a happy ritual—a celebration!"

The Raven, black as coal, was hopping up and down in glee. "Better them than us," he said as he burrowed into his tight, slick coat, plucking out an insect for his breakfast.

A pigeon, flying to rest on the Scarecrow's shoulder, startled him, almost causing him to topple over. In an instant, Chantecler spurted to the Scarecrow and held him up. Turning to the pigeon he gently admonished, "Be gentle, my friend. Our Scarecrow is much needed and we value him highly." The Scarecrow's face lit up and his frame took on a firmness reflecting his pride.

The pigeon, truly sorry for having jolted the Scarecrow, made his apologies. Now the bustling activities of the barnyard caught his attention and aroused his curiosity.

"Why is everyone so excited?" he asked.

"Because it is daybreak!", said Patou. "The dawn is risen and today is another new day!"

"That is true," replied the pigeon, "But there was a day yesterday, there is a day today, there will be another day tomorrow. There is a day each day!"

Chantecler winced, reminded of how much is taken for granted. It wasn't even done maliciously, he thought, but in innocence making it almost impossible to fight.

"Our visitor is a real dunce," said the Raven, condescendingly.

"You mustn't be unkind," Chantecler reprimanded.

He found the Raven difficult to tolerate at times. His humor was edged so sharply, it cut deeply. And because he spoke out of both sides of his mouth, one never quite knew where he stood. He always elevated his position by knocking someone else off of theirs. And he felt superior to everyone in the barnyard, including Chantecler, who was well aware of his envy. Lately, he had grown even more insolent and bold. Chantecler thought that this insolence, combined with his deviousness, would warrant a closer look.

But for the moment, Chantecler addressed himself to the pigeon, and without false modesty said, "It is with my song, dear friend, that I raise the sun!"

"And is your song special?" asked the pigeon.

"Yes," replied Chantecler with patience.

"And what makes it so special?" the pigeon continued innocently.

A loud commotion of cackling, cross talking, fluttering and stamping erupted, frightening the pigeon and causing him to move out of its range. He wondered what he had done to elicit such an unexpected response. A highly excitable, brown-speckled hen shouted, "That is a secret! A secret he has never, ever told anyone!"

Chantecler was touched, but also saddened. The intense curiosity surrounding his song had become a terrible burden. Because he was open, honest and direct, it went against his nature, and he had had to deal with those who thought it was an artificial contrivance in his throat that created the beauty and power of his song. Then there were those who ascribed it to a special ingredient in his corn, others to the actual spot where he sang. The most humiliating were those who simply called it magic. Yes, he thought, secrets were intolerable, for they carried the implication of rejection. Yet he knew some secrets must remain secret, for few could accept the truth in its nakedness.

The pigeon, more intrigued than ever by this mystery, asked a little skeptically, "But surely Chantecler, you have at the least told *your* hen!"

"His hens," he was quickly corrected by the others who felt insulted by the exclusion.

"You have more than one?" inquired the pigeon incredulously.

"He crows—remember you only coo," the Raven interjected.

"Then you are truly a most extraordinary rooster," the pigeon said in awe.

"When you praise him, call him the Cock!" reprimanded the white fulsome hen.

"His song is more an ornament to the landscape than the white hamlet to the hill!"

Chantecler was by no means modest, and while he was pleased with his hens for extolling his unusual virtues, he felt a slight embarrassment. To terminate the proceedings he jumped to the stone wall with a flourish and said, "Enough of this. The sun is risen. The day is in full bloom. To work now, all of you, with a will. Let us make labor a delight!"

Exhilarated, Chantecler's breast swelled to twice its size. His red mane graced his head like a crown and his beak jutted out like a rugged mountain. Yet his full white breast, firm as the stone wall he was standing on, seemed soft as down stuffed into a pillow.

"Let there be no idle quacking and pattering," he ordered. "You chickens, your task is to pick off slugs. You Cockerel, go practice your crow. I want to hear 'cock-a-doodle-do' four hundred times—and in hearing of the echo!"

As he continued his assignments, he heard grumbling among his hens, who felt put upon to do work other than the laying of eggs. I must keep their spirits up and their interest constant, he thought to himself. He knew happiness was a result of work, and that work was both purpose and privilege that gave meaning to life.

"Now," he said to the hens, "Walk among the roses and gobble every creature that threatens them. Ha! If the caterpillar thinks we will make him a gift of our flowers, he can stroke his belly—with his back! And you—go to the rescue of the cabbages, where grasshoppers lay siege to them with their battering rams!"

The pigeon was truly impressed with the absolute authority of Chantecler's leadership and all that he had heard. He could hardly contain his excitement. "How thrilled my mate will be to hear of the great Chantecler who will be remembered five, ten, even fifteen years from now," he exclaimed. "I must hurry home and tell her of my adventure and good fortune." He fluttered in mid-air for a second and was off, disappearing into the clear blue sky.

III

✥

The Escape

*N*o sooner had the pigeon departed than the sharp booming sound of a gun cracked across the barnyard like a bolt of lightning. Chantecler shivered and involuntarily stiffened up. Each time he heard this ugly sound he was filled with anger. He hated it more than anything else in the world. He could see its violent destruction in some poor creature unable to defend himself, and so was torn asunder.

Amidst the fear that had gripped the barnyard, Patou jumped up with a quiver and began scenting the air. "It's that old poacher again," he barked, beginning to drool.

The Raven, seeing that Patou was agreeably stimulated, seized the opportunity to wound him. "And you seem to love it unduly," he said.

"Yes," Patou responded honestly. Then

struck with remorse, he felt shamed. "I shall never resolve this terrible conflict," he cried out in despair. "My hunter's nostril twitches at the slightest shot, but my happiness here raises before me a bleeding wing, the glazed eye of a doe, the whimper of a rabbit's dying breath—and I feel the heart of a Saint Bernard waking in my breast!"

Chantecler felt the pain as his own. Under his influence, Patou had gone from a superb hunting dog to a civilized, domesticated friend. The clash had left him forever divided, so it was a constant battle to remain constrained. It had caused his face to droop, and later the expression came to be known as 'the hound dog look.'

"Relax, my good friend," Chantecler said compassionately, "It will soon pass in another moment."

But another shot rang out, closer and

more terrifying. Chantecler's feathers bristled, the sound reverberating in his head. A scream formed in his gut and he felt he was going to explode at any moment. "This is madness," he shouted in anger, "Sheer madness!"

Suddenly, flying over the wall in a panic and mad with fright, was a pheasant, beautiful beyond belief, with ruffled golden feathers that glittered brilliantly, creating a total aura around it. In its disarray it seemed possessed. "Help me! Please help me!" the pheasant screamed.

Chantecler was so struck by the perfect symmetry, the dazzling golden coat, the complete and utter beauty of this creature that he was blinded for the moment to its danger. Another shot rang out and the pheasant, out of its wits, ran to Chantecler, jumped into his outstretched wings and fainted. Chantecler was startled, his legs buckled momentarily, but he held the pheasant firmly.

He looked upon the reposed face with wonderment. He had seen many other beautiful creatures before, but this even surpassed the most beautiful. He noted the softness of the contours and that the heat from the pheasant's body had emitted a strong, exotic aroma.

He carried the pheasant to the water trough and scooped up a hand full of water. He hesitated a moment, unwilling to soil this most extraordinary countenance. Reluctantly, he saw no other course. As the pheasant revived, the nightmare of being pursued returned.

Madame Guinea Hen, unable to contain her curiosity and shaking with excitement, poked in close to them. "But how did you escape," she asked puzzled. The pheasant raised

her head slightly and said weakly, "The hunts-
man was surprised. He saw but a flash of gold
and I a flash of fire!" Then overcome by the
reminder, she cried out, "But the dog is chas-
ing me—a horrible dog!" Catching sight of
Patou from the side of her eye, she quickly
amended her speech. "I am not speaking of
you," she said, "but of the hunting dog."
Upset and agitated, the pheasant pleaded once
more, "Please! You must hide me before it's
too late!"

Chantecler carried the pheasant to
Patou's cottage, set it down gently and pushed
it in as far as he could, but no matter how he
arranged it, the pheasant's tail remained outside.

"There is too much of this golden vanity," said Patou, "I will have to sit on it."

Just then, the hunter's dog, with his long
ears banging against his face and his chops

quivering, came bounding into the barnyard, sniffing frantically. Patou greeted him calmly and Chantecler flattered him on his gentlemanly English manner. He could see that the hunter's dog was well disciplined and dedicated and that the pheasant would be lucky to survive.

"Have you seen a pheasant-hen go by?" he demanded.

"A pheasant-hen?", asked Patou astonished. "I have seen a pheasant, but certainly no pheasant hen!"

"That was she!" he confirmed.

Chantecler, equally as astounded as Patou, but puzzled, asked, "A pheasant-hen with golden plumage! But how can that be?"

"It is very rare," he answered, "But then it does happen. She sees the male in springtime putting on his holiday colors. He is so much more beautiful that she becomes jealous. It makes her mad! She then stops laying and hatching eggs and in turn nature gives her purple and gold—all the colors of the prism! So having shed the virtues of her sex—she flies freely forth!"

"In short," said Chantecler, "the pheasant your master missed was a she!" He thought this was strange, but he was sure there must be some ultimate purpose in it.

"Yes," said the hunter's dog, "and what a magnificent trophy it would have been. Not even I have ever seen a completely golden coat!"

A high-pitched whistle filled the air and the hunter's dog came to attention. He sniffed around, undetermined whether to try the area again or return immediately to his master. The whistle sounded again and he started off. The Raven called to him and he stopped abruptly.

Chantecler gasped in horror. What in

heaven's name can the Raven be thinking of, he thought. Is he possessed of some dark demon? It was so evil it repulsed him. He wondered how that poor creature, held prisoner in Patou's cottage, must feel. He was determined to deal with the Raven as soon as this danger had passed.

"You are losing something!" taunted the Raven.

The pheasant trembled beneath Patou, and he too vowed to make the Raven pay, should harm come to this frightened creature.

"Well, what is it?", asked the hunter's dog, impatiently.

"Time!", said the Raven, laughing, "You are losing time!"

The hunter's dog muttered angrily as he jumped the fence and returned to his master. A huge sigh of relief could be felt as the barnyard burst into a conglomeration of sounds.

There was jesting, and jokes were bandied about lightly, and as conjecture built, Chantecler hurried to Patou's kennel and indicated that he could rise.

IV

❦

The Discovery

The golden-pheasant emerged from the cottage, her feathers ruffled and on edge. She was furious, the anger bristling from every surface. She stood proud and defiant, her eyes like burning coals. She fixed on the Raven first. "That was a low, cruel jest," she said, "It was just what I would expect from an insensitive, pathetic soul of a Raven!" Then addressing the crowd, she stated, "Yes, it is true. I have rejected the male dominated tradition. You can belittle me if you will, but I am of great lineage, and proud as I am free. And when the roll is called, know that I am Claudine!"

"Whew! We hate ourselves, don't we?" said the Raven, sarcastically.

"I will never turn back!" she continued. "The golden tippet as I wear it curves and shimmers. The emerald epaulette articulating my shoulders acquires a shining grace. I have made of a mere uniform a miracle of style. Yes, it is true. I have stolen the dazzling plumage of the male. I will never turn back!"

Chantecler was stunned. She was not only beautiful, but at her core was a sense of individuality, of courage, of dignity and spirit. So much had happened so fast, he couldn't quite keep up with it. He knew he was irrevocably drawn to her, but he also sensed a danger which he rejected immediately.

Madam Guinea Hen was besides herself with joy at this show of independence. She too had always felt shafted and restrained by male tradition. She felt capable of leadership, and if not superior in many ways, was at least the equal of any male. Although she resisted in many subtle, indirect ways, she still felt a deep resentment. But in all honesty, she also knew she didn't have the courage, and so was thrilled by Claudine's stand.

"Bravo! Bravo!" she cried, "Oh my, my, my, my! You are really something special. And you are a great beauty, my dear, a great beauty! We must be friends! Oh, please, let us be friends!"

Claudine was charmed and honored by the approbation of Madame Guinea Hen and the other females. All of the attention gave her a sense of strength that was exhilarating. She noticed that Chantecler had changed imperceptibly. He had grown quiet, the look in his eye dark, and that he had taken a stance.

Madame Guinea Hen continued, requesting Claudine's presence as guest of honor at her cocktail party the next day. Out of the corner of her eye, Claudine could see that Chantecler had become cross. At that moment she resolved to accept the invitation.

"I am honored, Madam," she said "It will give me great pleasure to attend!"

Amid the squeals of delight, Chantecler stepped forward, bristling. They were purposely insubordinate, he thought, and even though his principles hadn't been stated formally, they were accepted code. And now they were being subverted. He felt his temperature rise and in trying to keep control of himself he felt the heft of his body increase. Unable to hold back the flush of heat, he said, "You will not attend!"

The moment he had uttered the order, he felt something had gone awry. He wished he could retrieve the words and bury them some place where they couldn't be found. The crowd became tense, moving back ever so slightly. The anticipation of a confrontation pervaded the air.

Claudine saw the consequences of his

challenge immediately. Should she back down, she would become a laughing stock. If she denied her statements, she would be considered hypocritical—a foolish old female. Yet, in his favor, he had saved her from the hunter's dog. Wasn't she obligated to save him, at the least, this awkwardness? No, she decided, as she recalled the past humiliations, I will not submit!

"So, you have made up my mind for me, have you!" she said, also taking a stance. "Does your male pose blind you to the fact that it is for just this reason that I have chosen to be free?"

Chantecler girded himself. She had thrown down the gauntlet, and now, as reluctant as he was, he had to stand firm.

"I will attend," she repeated emphatically. And then, as if to run the shibboleth through, she added, "And will you escort me?"

The impact of this thrust caught him completely off guard. He was astounded at her unmitigated gall, her unbelievable nerve. Yet, though he was appalled with her, he still had to admire her boldness. But the embarrassment was so keen he loudly said in indignation,

"No! I will not escort you! I will not attend!"

The Raven stepped in grandly and said, "Then please accept my invitation. We shall make a great pair. The light and the dark—so to speak!" He thought himself as handsome, in his way, as Chantecler and far more witty. He was sure Claudine would delight in his chivalry.

Chantecler fumed. He would have liked to take the Raven and thrash him to within an inch of his life. However, he knew that to do so would compound the error, and that he would appear even more petty and foolish so he remained silent.

Claudine turned on the Raven promptly, saying she didn't hold with those who made bad jests. The Raven felt he had been badly trapped. His humiliation was complete, but he remained composed, not wanting to give her any satisfaction. Lightly, almost flippantly, he chided, "Female and foolish!"

"Enough of all this," said Chantecler, relieved that an opportune moment had come to dissolve an ugly situation. "Night is coming!"

The crowds disbursed to their homes, except for the Raven and Claudine, who lingered near the stone wall. Chantecler stood his ground facing the Raven and said, "We shall meet directly, Raven! There seem to be differences that need resolving."

The Raven caught the sternness of his tone, and intimidated, left reluctantly. Retreat is the better part of valor, he thought. We shall meet again, but it will be on my terms!

V

Courtship

$\mathcal{C}$hantecler turned and at the sight of Claudine he forgot his irritation. Her beauty dissipated his remaining anger. The aura of her golden coat drew him closer as if hypnotized, and upon sensing her aroma, he fell under a spell. He remembered the softness of her form as he held her, the warmth that penetrated his arms, and the inviting stillness of her reposed face. A tremor took hold of him as the blood coursed to his loins. His head grew faint and he ached for her touch once again. His passion was rampant as he gently enfolded her with his wing.

She quickly removed herself from his embrace and wondered if this wasn't another of his approaches to subjugate her. "I know I am indebted to you, Chantecler," she said indignantly, "But if this is . . ."

"No! No!", he quickly assured her, "I

was simply offering you a token of my esteem! It is just that you are like a summer's breeze that brings with it the sweet scent of exotic flowers and the sensual caress of warmth. You are in your bountiful beauty like the splendor of royalty!"

As he spoke, he circled round, lowering one wing and then the other. The words cascaded down upon her like soft, floating leaves from a tree in fall. She started to feel faint, as if without a will of her own. But just as her lips were about to give their consent, she moved out of his circle, and recovering quickly, she stood off away.

"Yes, you do that quite nicely," she said, relieved. "But as you can see, it has had no effect at all!" I must keep him at a distance, she thought. He has a presence that is overwhelming. As Chantecler tried to move in closer, she held him off with more words.

"Oh, I know we are the illustrious Chantecler, and there isn't a hen alive who wouldn't preen her feathers for a moment's distraction. But as far as I am concerned, you are too frankly, Cock of the Walk!"

Chantecler, still on course, did not want to aggravate her further, so he remained silent, all the while thinking that it was true. He did have his choice of the hens whenever he wanted. On the other hand, that was the privilege of his position. And yet, he did show a concern for their needs as well. And when all was said and done, he was, in the bargain, irresistible. Lastly, he was in accord with nature in that variety was both the spice and the essence of life!

Claudine detected a vanity on his face that could not be concealed, so she continued her assault saying, "You are altogether too spoiled! The only cock to my fancy would be a plain, inglorious cock to whom I would be all in all. Do not take me for one of your barnyard hens!"

She had penetrated a most vulnerable spot and it stung him to the quick. He felt his anger rise, and unable to control his irritation his temper flared and he exploded. "Greatness is where greatness is found!" he said, "Just as beauty is where beauty is found!

Claudine, sensing victory and stimulated by the battle, bore down. "And do you think the world ends at your little vegetable patch?" she asked.

"No!", he replied.

"And, if you compared, would you concede that all these things around you are dreary, poor and flat?" she persisted.

The needling was like torture. "I will admit to personal vanity, but to attack my beloved barnyard is presumptuous and intolerable. I concede nothing," he said, "I can never become used to the richness and wonder of my world!"

You must agree," she said tenaciously, "It is always the same!"

"Nothing is ever the same—nothing—even under the sun! And that is because of the sun! For she changes everything," he exclaimed indignantly.

Claudine was taken aback. How dare he think of the sun as female, she fumed to herself. It is unfair. He has dealt unfairly with me! It was as if she had been given a blow to the midriff. She felt the balance turning against her, and breathless with anger and unable to reply more extensively said, "She—who!"

"Light, the universal goddess! You see that geranium planted by the farmer's wife? It is never twice the same red. And that pitchfork standing in the corner dozing and dreaming of hay fields- unique! And that old shoe spurting straw—what a sight—what a beautiful sight! Nothing I tell you is two instants the same! And because of her, the glory of things is such that I fall into startled admiration and my eye grows round!"

Suddenly, Claudine's gaze became fixed by his speech. It was common, she thought, but so infused with sincerity and love that it took wing as poetry. He even seemed to transcend his male ego, pointing to a hidden depth. She grew pensive and tender. "One feels you have a soul," she said.

Chantecler became calm after his last outburst. Although he was spent, a trace of anger remained. He was surprised at her tenderness, but wary that it might be capricious. He tried sounding a bit more conciliatory.

"Anyone, Claudine, with the power to see and the capacity to suffer may come to understand all things. In an insect's death are hinted disasters. And through a knot-hole one can see the sky and marching stars!"

Darkness had fallen and the silence was so still, that all that could be heard was the beat of their hearts. And this was more felt than heard. The sense of intimacy was profound.

"Then . . . you . . . love me . . . it seems," she said tenderly.

"Yes," he said, his heart pounding furiously.

Throwing caution to the wind, he embraced her. "From the first moment that I saw you I was so taken by your beauty I have not been the same. And when I discovered you were a woman, I became wild with desire!"

"And how much do you love?" she asked.

"With everything that is me," he said. "I

had made up my mind that should the hunter's dog have discovered you, he would have had to take you over my dead body."

"Then your love has no limits," she said.

"None," he replied.

He embraced her again and they kissed. She was so soft and warm to his touch he drew her as close as he could. The blood rampaged through him like a raging river violently trying to burst the banks of its containment. As her sweet smell reached his nostrils, he felt his head spin in a circle, faster and faster. He wanted desperately to possess her.

She withdrew from him slightly, yet remaining within his embrace, and looking into his eyes said, "Then you would have no objection to sharing the secret of your song with me?"

Chantecler stepped back, thunderstruck. He was immediately thrown into turmoil, split between confusion and repulsion. How could she ask this of him, he thought, angrily. How could she shatter this beautiful moment so near consummation? Was this the general condition of female pheasants? Or was it her particular design? His suspicion grew.

"Objection!" he said indignantly. "It is impossible! I have never told anyone my secret!"

"I see," she said, stepping further back.

"But why should that be a condition of our love?" he questioned.

"It would bind us in a way that no other can. It contains a total trust and loyalty—it would make our love complete!" she said.

Chantecler stood dazed, genuinely confused and torn. He wanted her at this moment more than anything else, but at this cost, it would be impossible, he reasoned. Should she know his secret would she still love him? Why this demand now he thought. His indignation rose again, and unable to restrain it he said, "No, I cannot do it! I can't reveal my secret! I have never ever told anyone! It is impossible!"

"Then your love does have limits," she said.

"Yes—no—," he stammered.

"Then so be it," she said with finality. "It is late and I am exhausted!"

She turned and headed for the shelter situated next to Patou's cottage. Chantecler stood there silently as night descended heavily, casting everything in such a dark pall that the air became stifling. Weary, he made his way to the barn, found his spot, and tried to sleep.

VI

―――――

The Night
Animals

*D*ark, deep night swallowed the last few sparks from the stars. A shadow had hidden the moon, so that not even a ghostly reflection remained. The Power of Night was everywhere with silence as its companion.

At a spot some distance from the barnyard, heaped with stones, pieces of broken pots, faggots, and covered with damp moss and ferns, there appeared two green, glowing circles floating ominously in the black miasma.

A thick, low, distorted moaning seeped through the blackness, desperately trying to free itself from some unseen bondage. Suddenly, two phosphorescent pulses, pale and ghostly, joined the erratic beat.

Then a deep, hollow, amorphous vibration quivered, gradually becoming a strangled cry that quickly subsided, fusing itself to the low moaning.

Two diamond blue glints appeared in the emptiness, refracting in all directions. And in quick succession, the space filled with an amber glow, a pale turquoise radiation, a ray of piercing violet, a flash of yellow and a spark of crimson, and in an explosion of silver, a phantomlike aura descended, creating a kaleidoscopic specter of evil.

Tortured, twisted uttering began to rise in phantom tones grouped together ghoulishly, reverberating eerily.

The Scarecrow, exhausted from the tension and excitement of the day, had gone to the field to reflect. He had sensed an uneasiness, and a foreboding had come over him. Tired, he had fallen asleep, until a shapeless monster, twisting and turning, sounded a deathlike tone that magnified to a shriek.

He awoke with a start and shook the sleep from his head, but the moaning persisted. Looking into the dark, he realized that it was coming from nearby and that it was real. He quietly inched his way toward the source and as he came closer he could see glow upon glow of color.

He concentrated his stare and as he brought everything into focus the shock hit him like a crackling bolt of lightning. He shivered and a cold tremble ripped through him. He could hardly believe what he saw. There were eyes! They were everywhere! The light from them multiplied until from their glare could be discerned a cat crouching on the grass, a mole clinging to a mossy stone. There were night birds of all sorts and sizes perched everywhere and forming a great circle!

In the center stood a huge mass with pointed ears, and eyes sunk deep into his head, glowing like red hot coals. He spread his wings, which spanned an entire branch. His talons cut deep into the bark with razor sharpness. He was so grotesque, his distortion seemed totally malevolent.

The Grand Duke known as The Prince of Night called the meeting to order. In a deep, resonant voice, intense and sinister, he intoned, "Before we begin, let us give the cry which makes us all one!"

The weird, ghoulish moaning the Scarecrow had heard became a rumble, and then a roar. It exploded into an articulation filled with loathing and hatred. In unison, they shouted

CHANTECLER MUST DIE!
CHANTECLER MUST DIE!

CHANTECLER MUST DIE!
LONG LIVE THE NIGHT!
LONG LIVE THE NIGHT!
LONG LIVE THE NIGHT!

The Scarecrow, although riddled through with fear, moved closer to the broken stone wall and still trembling, concealed himself between two boulders. He could see the Screech Owl, the Wood Owl, the Old Horned Owl, several of the bats, and the cat and the mole. He knew them well, for they had pecked and scratched at him when he hung in the field. To see them all together made him shudder. He wondered what common purpose they had.

As the Grand Duke called the roll, checking off attendance, each of the assembled creatures shouted their hatred of Chantecler. The cat hated him because he loved the dog Patou. The mole, because he had never seen him. An owl because he wasn't web-footed and marked his passage by a track of stars. But the deep, underlying hatred that unified them all was engendered because Chantecler brought the day that temporarily ended their lives. Light was their mortal enemy. It drove them underground and into hiding. And it was Chantecler who inexorably brought this torment.

An alien sound caught the Grand Duke's attention. In a moment all eyes turned toward it. The Scarecrow leaned forward and strained with all his might to see the figure. To his amazement, he saw it was the Raven, hopping up and down. What in the world is he doing here? he wondered. He is in mortal danger! No sooner had the thought emerged than a great screeching and howling gripped the night. With talons outstretched and eyes glowering, the wild assortment of birds surrounded the Raven menacingly. The Grand Duke ordered him upon pain of death to identify himself promptly and state his purpose.

The Raven felt a cold clamminess pass over him. He knew they could tear him to shreds and dispose of him in seconds if they struck. If he showed the least fear they would pounce immediately.

"I am the Raven," he said calmly, trying hard to suppress the tremor in his voice.

"You are from the other world," accused the Grand Duke.

"Yes and no," replied the Raven. And then to throw them off, added flippantly, "I am here in the artist's spirit to look on without taking sides.

An owl asserted that if he wasn't taking sides that meant he was siding with them. The Raven thought this a primitive notion. Another owl then concluded the opposite, that if he wasn't with them, he was against them. The Raven, regaining his composure and growing more bold, jested, pointing out that the owl was seeing with only one eye while there were always two sides.

The Grand Duke was indignant. "There is only once source- one light," he exclaimed, "And there is only one Chantecler! And as soon as that Cock has sounded—everything becomes temporary!"

The Barn Owl poked his head forward and added, "And though the Night be still black, we are painfully aware of it growing less and less black!"

The Old Horned Owl moved in danger-ously close to the Raven, and trembling, he said, "When his metallic voice has cleft the night, we squirm like worms in a fruit that is cut in two!"

The Raven, detecting their fear, grew insolent. He belittled the Old Horned Owl saying, "Just because he brings the light doesn't . . ."

Before he could finish, the birds attacked him violently. As the Scarecrow watched, his heart beat rapidly. His impulse was to try and help the Raven, but prudence prevailed. There were just too many of them, and they would tear him to shreds.

"Never speak that word!" warned the Grand Duke, addressing the Raven sternly.

The Raven apologized and in trying to explain what he had meant, he inadvertently said, "But the brightness . . . ."

They all retreated in dismay, pained to the core. The word was like a slashing whip. The Old Horned Owl then moved forward aggressively and said, "Never utter that horrible, grating word that so hatefully suggests the scratching of a match."

But the Raven was as perverse as he was

obstinate, and in trying to justify his blunder, he said, "But the day . . ."

Again they jumped on him, pummeling and scratching, all the while shouting, "He comes to torment us! He is with Chantecler! Kill him!"

The Raven, bruised and disheveled, shook himself loose from their grip and pleaded, "Please! Please! You are mistaken! I am with you! I am one of you! I am as wicked, as despicable, as evil as you! Please give me a chance to explain!"

The Grand Duke called them off and turning to the Raven told him it had better be good as death was but a breath away.

The Raven told how in his previous life he was a slimy, slithering creature and whatever he touched he corrupted, turning it to decay and stench. He feared no deities, his duty being to reveal the deep, hidden rot, the deceit and cowardice that hid behind cloaked faces. He rejoiced in killing for killing's sake, even his mother, his wife, his children! And now, his singular passion was to see the dreaded Chantecler dead! Evil was his constant companion! Yes! He was one of them—dark, devious and craven!

His tirade was so intense it became an evangelistic spirit. The more he railed, the more persuasive he became until he had inflamed their passion to such a degree they hoisted him to their shoulders and declared him one of them!

The Scarecrow was horrified. Could the Raven have performed so realistically just to save his skin or was it true that he was reincarnated? He had heard of the supernatural before, but had paid no mind to it as it seemed virtually impossible to realize. As their ritual grew more wild and bizarre he wanted to alert

Chantecler, but the thought of being detected made him stay put.

The Grand Duke was delighted to add a kindred spirit and an ally, for evil needed constant refueling to create larger and larger fields of influence. Despite what others thought, evil did not come naturally. It had to be taught, encouraged, reinforced, and inspired. Consequently, he was grateful for all the help he could get.

The Raven, starting out just to play the game, had come to within a hair's breath of death. But having had to reveal his inner self, and for once moving off center, he now felt cleansed in the admission of his true evilness. He was high with excitement and free of any guilt. The ecstasy was almost unbearable. The crucible of danger had made him whole! Together they would conquer the world!

The Grand Duke called for order. "The

time is short," he said, "And as you know, it is not sufficient to just think evil. All the world thinks evil. However, to be truly great falls only to those who are able to execute evil. That is what separates us from them!

The Old Horned Owl stepped forward and told of how he had flown to a farm six lengths away, and scaring the farmer's daughter had caused her to loose the gates holding the great fighting cocks of the world. He described how their master has fastened two razor blades to the heels of the great champion—The White Pile!

"He will be dead by tomorrow," gloated the Grand Duke. "The fighting cocks are to be honored at Madam Guinea Hen's party where they will meet Chantecler. They will pick his eyes out of his sockets!"

The Raven jumped to a higher branch so

that he would be more visible. "He is not going," he said, "Chantecler has refused!"

A surge of depression engulfed the gathering. They had been foiled before and the frustration had mounted to where it verged on insanity.

"Don't despair," encouraged the Raven, "Knowing Chantecler as I do, I would surely go straight to the Cock and tell him!"

The Grand Duke frowned and thought the Raven had taken leave of his senses. "Tell him?" he asked angrily. "What sort of jest is that!"

The rebuke was so stern that the others took it as a signal to surround the Raven for a possible kill. He tried growing smaller, but there was nowhere to hide.

"But surely you must know," he said quickly, "that the brave are seldom prudent.

Chantecler shrinks from no challenge! He counts that quality among his greatness!"

The Grand Duke was mollified for the moment and softened his expression, growing thoughtful. "All right," he said, "Let us suppose him going then."

The Raven was again center stage. He felt their concentration on his pending words exhilarating. He liked to be important. And as he thought of Chantecler's death, he gained a new boldness.

"Chantecler, for all his fame has retained his bluff frankness," continued the Raven. "When he sees the contortions of those snobs he is sure to say things which they are equally sure to take up. In other words, he will provoke the fight!"

The Grand Duke immediately saw the accuracy of this psychological insight and was struck by the Raven's brilliance. "Very well done," he replied. "That is a master stroke." The others took their cue from the Grand Duke and joined in exclamations of ingenious, beautiful, fantastic! Then in a burst of enthusiasm they hoisted the Raven to their shoulders and gave a mighty cheer.

Suddenly, the Grand Duke retreated in utter pain. As he covered his eyes with his wings, he shrieked with despair. "Time has slipped! Our night—our glorious night- is torn from us, for even before a sound is sounded, I hear it coming! Quickly, let us give our cry!"

"Chantecler must die!" shouted the Grand Duke

"Chantecler must die!" they joined.

"Chantecler will die!" he led.

"Chantecler will die! they repeated.

Then in unison they gave their long last cry:

LONG LIVE THE NIGHT!
LONG LIVE THE NIGHT!

In a moment they had all dispersed, except for the Raven. How ignoble, he thought, to have suffered in this way. Soon it would end. Scores would be settled and the last laugh would be his. He, too, would be remembered fifty, a hundred, maybe two hundred years! The Raven approached the Scarecrow's spot, but he was so preoccupied with grandeur that he walked right by as if blinded.

The Scarecrow breathed a sigh of relief. His first impulse was to run and tell Chantecler of his danger, but immediately upon this thought, the realization dawned that should he inform Chantecler, the reaction might be just as the Raven wished. As he pondered this dilemma, its complexity rested heavy upon him. Totally exhausted, he fell off to sleep.

VII

✻

The Secret

Chantecler awoke with a fright, worried that he had missed his time to call the sun and start the dawning. He looked around and was relieved to see the blackness. His inner, intuitive clock had once again performed well. It always told him, long before there was any evidence, that day was approaching. However, he had slept badly, tossing and turning, all the while puzzling over Claudine. When he had dozed off, it was a deep, concentrated slumber that almost caused him to miss his proper sign.

He roused himself, brushed away the remaining languor, and hurried along the path to a favorite spot that seemed to enrich his song. His perplexity still clung to him. Why was she challenging him? Why did she oppose him? Why was she so unreasonable as to suppose he would reveal his secret? Why was she so obstinate? Question after question tumbled out in a torrent. Yet, as his anger rose, so did his desire for her, until it became a throbbing ache that constantly asserted itself.

He was so preoccupied, he had not noticed the presence ahead. Just as he was about to collide with it, a voice startled him back to reality. It was Claudine.

"Chantecler!" she said, alarmed. "You seemed intent on trampling me!"

"But what are you doing out?" he said, surprised. "It is still dark and the dawn is some way off!"

"I could not sleep well. I have had a wretched night!" she complained.

Like Chantecler, she had gone to bed, but had not slept. She could not understand why he had to be so dominant, why he opposed her being honored, why he wouldn't share his secret, particularly since he said he loved her.

There were so many unanswered questions that in her bewilderment she took to the path for some fresh air and tried to escape their irritation.

"I am truly sorry," Chantecler said sincerely, as he began to move toward his spot. "I was caught unawares and now I must hasten to call the sun. You can walk with me if you wish."

She hesitated for a moment, then decided to accompany him. She would watch him closely for the clue to his secret. In the process she would see a dawning being made at first hand. She was sure the experience would be instructive and possibly even inspirational.

Chantecler felt encouraged by her sign of acquiescence, and as she hurried to keep stride with him, he asked, "Are you still going to attend Madame Guinea Hen's party?"

"Yes," she replied, catching up to him. "That is the purpose for which I stayed over."

Chantecler picked up his pace somewhat, so that Claudine had to quicken her speed. She wasn't quite sure whether his hurrying was due to duty or in response to her answer.

"And will you accompany me?" she tested, hoping that his sentiments had changed.

Again he sped up, refusing her invitation. He told her it would be weak, a betrayal of his beliefs, and that it would have an adverse effect on the barnyard.

He takes himself so seriously, she thought, and he is so obstinate. He just won't give an inch. There is no reasoning with him. Then in an instant, she was hit with an inspiration. She would use her feminine wiles. So as she walked, she placed herself in the proper position, tripped and fell forward. Just as she was about to hit the ground, Chantecler grabbed for her and drew her close. She put her arms around him and embraced him tightly, allowing her softness and warmth to penetrate. She could feel him respond, and looking into his eyes, she said seductively,

"It is not a weakness I feel here in your arms, but a strength! And it would be quite a measure were you to accompany me to the party . . . and surely greatness were you to share your secret!"

Chantecler broke his embrace and stepped back indignantly. As he did, he realized he had arrived at his destination. There was much work to be done and time was short. But thoughts of her jostled him. Why does she torment me with her touch? Why does she lull me with the sensuous honey of her sound? Why does she persist so tenaciously?

81

"I will never tell my secret," he said adamantly.

Claudine, ever more determined, moved in closer to him, preening her golden coat so that its softness was inviting. However, Chantecler turned away.

"Come now," she said, "Look at me. Look into my eyes. She gently turned him toward her and continued. "I know Chantecler . . . I know that in your heart of hearts, you do want to tell me—you do want to share your secret!"

It was true, he thought, I do want to unburden myself. But how does she see inside my heart? Is it so clearly written on my face or does she have some special intuitive power? No, it is obvious, she thinks I am a fool easily led by her sex appeal!

"And if I told you my secret," he said angrily, "Could you then raise the sun too?"

"That is not my purpose," she replied.

"Then why must you know?" he asked.

Claudine felt her anger rise with his sharpness. She struggled to maintain her composure "Why do you mock me? Is it because you do magic?" she asked calmly.

"Magic!" he replied disdainfully. "Magic will never make the sun rise or fall, because it is hocus-pocus! It is only by nature's law with its causes and effects that I make the sun heed my call!"

He began to clear the ground of stones and weeds. He worked furiously until the soft, rich earth shone through. His efforts were so strenuous, Claudine grew concerned for his well being.

"The waves of sound are so high nobody can hear," he shouted in another burst of energy. "I spread my wings to feel out for their song. Then magnetic lines of force beat out like a drum. The force comes down from the north and up from the south until it converges at my feet! Then finding that particular locus—plus or minus a second—and when the forces focus, I sing!"

Chantecler dug his claws into the earth. He unloosed them, then felt around for a better position. Once again, he gripped the soil firmly. His breath had become short and his face flushed.

"You will kill yourself, Chantecler," Claudine said, deeply alarmed. "You must stop!"

"Never," he shouted. "It is when I am giving, when I am doing my duty, when I am killing myself that I live most completely!"

He was so possessed, she could not take her eyes off of him. It was as if he had bound her with an invisible cord. She wondered what fury she had unleashed in him. She stood terrified and fascinated at the same time.

Chantecler took a deep breath and held it for what seemed an eternity. His body expanded to twice its size. Every muscle was taut and stretched to its limit. His face was a deep red, the veins pounding furiously.

"He is killing himself," she cried. "Why did I push him so far? Why did I insist?" As regret followed regret, she was overwhelmed with guilt.

Chantecler then let loose with his first sound. It began with a narrow force, then broadened out into a triangle until it soared into the blackness like an explosive missile. The roar was so gigantic he fell back from the impact of the sound.

Claudine rushed to him, but he held her away with outstretched arms. He immediately began to dig his claws into the earth again. As he was preparing, Claudine discovered dark turning to blue. In her excitement she shouted to him.

"I see a dawning! The sky is no longer dark! And the star is extinguished!"

"I extinguished nothing," he corrected. "The star has veiled itself. Even in daylight the stars are there!'"

He took several short breaths and then a larger breath. His breast grew round, his eyes intense. In his mind's eye he could envision his song. He held his breath until his muscles ached with such pain, that he thought they would tear into a million pieces. And then with a resounding force, his sound exploded over the entire valley.

The light blue turned green, and the green turned orange. Claudine was beside herself with excitement. When the yellow among the pine trees shone, she exclaimed in awe,

"It is yellow!"

"Gold," Chantecler said, disappointed. "It should be gold!"

"And I see pearly gray," Claudine added quickly

"It shall be white!" he affirmed. "I am far from finished!"

"As object after object lifted its veil, Claudine became entranced. "Every hollow in every tree is as pink as a wild rose," she said, particularly touched by this sight.

Her response took him so off guard, he felt inspired to new heights. "As I sense love in addition to faith, I say the Day today shall be more beautiful than ever!"

Claudine felt lured into an irresistible vision, and persuaded by what she considered his madness said, "Yes, love is involved in the mystery!"

"It is more than a mystery, Sweet Heart,"

he said. "It is a sacred thing you are witnessing. It is a sacred thing into which I am initiating you!"

Chantecler prepared the earth. When he sensed the right moment, he held firmly. He saw Claudine, and the anticipation in her eyes moved him deeply.

"Come closer," he said. "You help me to sing better. Collaborate!"

Claudine sprung to his side, and beaming with joy she exclaimed, "I love you!"

"Every word you whisper in my ear shall be translated into sunshine for all the world to see!" he replied.

"I love you!," she repeated fervently.

"Say it again, and I will gild the mountain suddenly," he urged.

"I love you!" she said wildly. "Let me see you gild it!"

Chantecler sung with inspiration. His call

was bold, sensuous, sonorous and compelling. The mountain turned gold.

"I can see your work growing! It is growing everywhere!" she cried.

"I can see it in your eyes," he said, finding new strength.

Claudine pressed herself closer to his side, her eyes glowing with ecstasy.

"I am proud of you Chantecler!" she said.

"I am at once doing my duty and making you more fair! Men offer trinkets, but I wreaths and halos of glitter. I offer the dawn!

The sky grew dark and a pall seemed to settle. Claudine jumped up in a panic and screamed, "Chantecler, it is slipping. It is slipping away!"

Chantecler dug into the earth, desperately trying to find his position. He trembled with fear that he would not be in time. He took several quick breaths of air, held them in until he started to grow, and when he felt as if he were about to die, he let his song soar into the sky and over the valley. The clouds shook as if rattled by a giant and the sun burst through with a brilliance beyond belief. It was the most magnificent he had ever called forth!

Claudine was overwhelmed with amazement. She felt a reverence so profound she began to tremble.

"The sun," she exclaimed, "You have brought the sun in all its splendor!"

Chantecler felt his head whirl, his vision blur. He fell to the ground exhausted. He lay still, his heart pounding wildly. Claudine rushed to his side, lifted his head onto her arms and wiped his brow.

"You are spent, my love," she said tenderly. "You must rest and gather your strength!"

Chantecler reached out aimlessly and tried to right himself.

"Help me," he pleaded. "This is a dreadful moment! No sooner does my reason return than I go mad!"

"Hush now, my dear. Stay calm in my arms!"

"I made the sunrise," he shouted madly, then overcome with despair, "Oh, what shall I do Claudine?"

"What is it my love?" she asked sadly.

"Were you to know, will you promise never to tell my enemies?," he asked.

"Chantecler, my own! I could never speak against you. I would not break my own heart. Rest easy, tell me your pain," she said.

Chantecler told her of his anguish. He explained how making the sun rise each day was a terrible burden of responsibility. That he felt the future depended on something which might fail. That he was never sure, when the day was ready, to find his song. That his song remained a mystery to him, that it did not come by rote, but by a creative effort that he was never sure he could duplicate. And that was why some days were gray, some overcast, and some blessed with brilliance.

"Then your secret is no secret and all," she said stunned.

"My secret is that each new day requires a totally new creative effort that I am never sure of reaching," he explained.

Claudine, realizing the depth of his anguish, gently placed his head to her breast.

"You will find it," she reassured him, "You will surely find it always!"

"Yes, talk to me like that. I listen. I need you. You must always believe me when I believe," he pleaded, "And never when I doubt. Tell me again!"

"You are beautiful," she said, rocking him back and forth.

"I care nothing for that," he said stirring.

"You sang beautifully," she tried to reassure him.

"Say that I sang badly, but tell me that it is I who . . .," he cried out, but Claudine cut him off.

"Yes! Yes! I admire you beyond all bounds and measure!" she said quickly.

"No," he said, frustrated. "Tell me that what I told you is true!"

"Yes, dear Chantecler," she said stroking his forehead. "Yes, my glorious beloved, it is you who make the dawn appear!"

Chantecler lay still against her breast as Claudine continued to stroke his forehead. Gradually, with each gentle touch, he felt the tension begin to dissipate and a calmness return.

How wonderful it is, she reflected. The great Chantecler needs me. He asked me to collaborate! And together we raised the sun. It was fantastically thrilling. It was even grander than when I took my colors from the male. And now he loves me! He has proven it by sharing his secret. He looked so magnificent when doing his duty, ardent, inspiring, electrifying. And now, here in my arms he was so vulnerable I simply wanted to protect and mother him. How truly remarkable it had been, she thought, to have gone from near death yesterday to the supreme heights today. Life was a wonder!

VIII

❧

The Raven's Deception

The Raven had left the meeting of the Night Animals determined to execute evil! He had canvassed the area trying to find Chantecler, and when the first sound of Chantecler's song pierced the night, he determined its general direction, fixed a radius, and made his way to it guided by its increasing intensity. Soon, he thought, all accounts would be settled. His ordeal under fire had given him a sense of rebirth. For the first time he felt he had an identity that was clearly defined and precise. He was evil and he loved it! The banishment of guilt made him feel powerful and the approbation of his peers stimulated him to action. As he came upon Chantecler and Claudine in embrace, he saw their obvious love. He had moved stealthily, so that when he jumped out from behind the tree, they were startled.

97

"Ah ha," he said mockingly. "The two love birds. One, two, three . . . instant love. Very modern indeed!"

Chantecler was aghast, concerned that the Raven had overheard his secret. Claudine felt him tremble and held him securely, calming his alarm.

"Where have you come from?" he asked tremulously.

"Through a dream darkly. Actually, I was out for an early snack," he replied.

"It seems more like eavesdropping," said Chantecler infuriated.

"Then half the world must be looking in, for I also heard the sparrows chatting, the hens pecking, and I saw the Scarecrow waking, rather late, I thought!"

The Scarecrow had slept soundly, escaping the emotional turmoil that had exhausted him. But once awake, he was overcome by guilt. He felt he had wasted time and had kept Chantecler in jeopardy of his life. Upon reflection, he had decided to tell him of the plot, regardless of the consequences. He would trust in Chantecler's wisdom to do the right thing. He moved quickly from the field to a better vantage point higher up. He recalled hearing Chantecler's call, but could not determine whether it had sounded just in his dream. Trusting his intuition, he urgently set off to the east of the field.

"Isn't this your big day?" the Raven asked Claudine. "I seem to remember you are to be honored today."

"I have already been honored, far beyond anything I could have anticipated," she informed him proudly.

Chantecler became immediately alarmed. He had seen the Raven provoke many others into saying things they wished had remained unspoken. He was masterful and experienced and counted these abilities among his greatest accomplishments. Chantecler signaled Claudine frantically with his eyes, but she became engrossed in countering the Raven. Finally, unable to control his fear, he gave her an obvious sign, which the Raven detected promptly.

"I see," he said, "Love's secrets. Yes, of course, we mustn't broadcast it to the world. How very compromising it would be!"

Claudine was offended by the Raven's presumption. He was reducing a beautifully ennobling experience to the level of the flesh and the commonplace. As she was about to chastise Raven, she saw the Scarecrow running toward them in the distance. He tripped and fell, picked himself up and continued, then stumbled again, and by the time he arrived he was huffing and puffing. Upon seeing the Raven, he became frightened and scurried behind Chantecler. Trembling, he tried to hide, but Chantecler brought him forward and close to him. He put his arms around him and said,

"You seem in mortal danger, my friend. Tell me, what can it be?"

"An empty head," jested the Raven.

"You are consistently yourself," admonished Claudine. "A bad jest at a bad time. Don't you see he is terrified?"

"Come now Scarecrow. We shall protect you," Chantecler assured him. "But you must tell us what danger there is."

The Scarecrow had focused his eyes on the Raven without varying them for a moment. Chantecler looked at him, then the Raven, puzzled as to the connection there might be between them.

"Is the Raven involved?" he inquired.

101

The Scarecrow was immobile, but nodded his head ever so imperceptibly. Claudine went over to him, gently put her hand on his face, and stroked him.

"No danger will harm you, dear one," she said. "Tell us what you know and we will help you."

The Scarecrow took a deep breath and blurted out what he had seen during the night. Chantecler turned to the Raven, enraged, and asked,

"Is that true Raven? Do you associate with those who hate me?"

"Of course I was there," replied the Raven, "But in the spirit of the artist. I simply observe, the better to render a true portrait."

"Is that all you have to say or are you just blowing air?" Chantecler demanded.

"Very well," said the Raven piqued,

"There are those who resent your attitude of 'I'm the whole show."

"I see," he replied. "Your friends are of small mind, small ambition, and small accomplishment; so they must congregate in darkness to gain stature!"

"You leave no room for tolerance," he said, "As to my taste in friendship, I say to each his own!"

"No, you pitiful jester. The habit for deception has grown so strong, you can no more be in earnest about friendship now than about anything else," he said, raising his voice. "Who are my enemies?"

"The owls," replied the Raven, stepping back a little.

"You sorry fool," Chantecler said, "Can't you see that greatness is often measured by the hatred of one's enemies? Because the owls are against me my destiny is inevitable!"

"Rest easy then," said the Raven lightly, "For they have a deal on—your lighting the world being a trifle flashy for their taste—a deal on for cutting your throat!"

The Scarecrow went faint. What should he do? he thought. He looked at Claudine imploringly. She too was alarmed, but also bewildered, not knowing where this exchange would lead. The Scarecrow summoned his courage and said,

"Yes, Chantecler. What he says is true. You are in danger! But . . ."

The Raven cut him short saying, "Although he is empty headed and subject to imaginary visions, I believe he has seen the true danger, accurately."

"And who is suppose to cut my throat?" questioned Chantecler.

"A brother bird," replied the Raven. "A Cock, born and bred to cockfighting, with razors attached to his heels. A champion of champions. He is known the world over as The White Pile! And he is to meet you at Madam Guinea's party."

Claudine sighed with relief. Chantecler was adamant about not attending, and the decision was fully reinforced by his principles. How glad she was now that he had refused to accompany her.

Chantecler turned and started toward the west field. Claudine ran to him and placed her body in front of his.

"Where are you going?" she asked, panicked.

"To the Guinea Hen's," he said emphatically.

"No! You mustn't go!" she cried.

"We shall!" he said absolutely determined.

"We can't," repeated Claudine, "I fear for your safety!"

"Yes, I heartily agree," taunted the Raven. "Take my advice, don't go. He could make two bites of either you or me!"

The Scarecrow was horrified to see the evil plan proceeding just as the Night Animals had set it up. The Raven was diabolical in his accurate perception of Chantecler's psyche, and the incredible way he was manipulating it. Desperate to stop it, he screamed out to Chantecler.

"Your response is precisely what they predicted! It is part of their plan to provoke you. You must not go. I beg you!"

"Please, Chantecler, for my sake, let us refrain," she pleaded.

"No! To do so would be cowardly," he replied.

"And do you wear your courage on your sleeve?" she asked plaintively.

"I see courage as a constant challenge," he replied, "that must be exercised to be vigorous and filled with life!"

"Don't say you haven't been warned," gloated the Raven in triumph.

"Forewarned is to be forearmed," Chantecler said jauntily. "Come, my dear, do not let this silly bird frighten you. Let us turn this party into a celebration!"

Claudine plummeted to an emotional depth never before experienced. Her premonition was so dark it devoured the joy she had felt only moments ago. The speed at which events were happening was so fast, it was like riding a whirlwind that tossed and turned, threatening to hurl the chosen subject into infinity, and breaking it to pieces by its force.

As the Scarecrow watched them disappear, he too, was wretched and racked with guilt. If he had not slept he would have been able to get to Chantecler first. He might have prevented this dreadful outcome. He deserved to be ignored, he thought. I am empty, useless, and might as well have never been made!

The Raven, enjoying his triumph, approached the Scarecrow and pecked a straw from him.

"Be careful you foolish bag of straw, that a strong wind doesn't blow your brains away," he warned. And then he flew off to the impending fireworks.

The Scarecrow followed dejectedly. Maybe he could redeem himself, he thought. He would watch and should the need arise he would throw himself between the fighting cocks and Chantecler!

IX

Madam Guinea Hen's Party

At the back of the barn, which was some distance from the farmer's house, lay an expanse of grass, graced by a large tree that had seen many years of life. The tree was a resting place for some, a retreat for others, and shade from the summer heat for many. For Madame Guinea Hen, it was the ideal place to hold her legendary parties, which were known far and wide.

Her parties set the fashion. They conferred status, and although they were artificial they still had validity among the ambitious and the pretentious. One was considered "in or out" of society by their attendance, or chic, or witty, or brilliant. Her invitations were so coveted the invitee would go to great lengths to attend. Some borrowed heavily to make the right appearance, some boned up on various subjects of conversation, some attended other smaller events so as to have prior status, and still others dug for the latest gossip to appear current.

An underlying viciousness lay at the foundation of her parties. Reputations could be made or lost depending on one's response to the acerbic or pseudo smart remarks. An expensive costume could be reduced to shreds with small, cutting jibes. Innuendoes could shatter years of work spent building one's standing in that community. Gossip was so thick and furious it was like a swarm of wasps. The scramble for approbation, applause, acclaim, fame and celebrity, was so incessant, it was fought over at any cost.

The fact that the fabulously beautiful Claudine was to be the guest of honor had made this party a success d'estime before one drink had been drunk, one hors d'oeuvre eaten, or one witticism expressed.

With word that the fighting cocks of the world were also to attend, the information had traveled like a whirlwind on a rampage, and caused a stampede for the few openings that remained

The sun was high and brilliant and illuminated the arrivals, which had begun early with the goose, the gander, the turkey-hen, the duck, the tufted-hen, the peacock, the pigeon, the young guinea cock, the swan, the cat, the pig, and a hundred others. As the Magpie stood by the entrance, a roadway leading to the farmer's barnyard, and announced each new arrival. a buzz of excitement would arise.

Standing off in the corner was the Raven holding court with his rapid fire witticism that raised scattered titters. The peacock assumed a position of display and spread his tail into a kaleidoscope of brilliant colors that created a chorus of Oh's and Ah's.

In another corner lay Patou, growling angrily under his breath. He too had heard of the fighting cocks, but despite his revulsion concerning these parties (he and Chantecler were one on this matter), he had attended to make sure that no unfair advantage was taken of Chantecler should he attend. He had hoped wisdom would prevail, but he knew how stubborn Chantecler could be, and given a challenge to his courage, would not back down.

The Scarecrow lay propped against a stone next to Patou. He had related the course of events to Patou, who could only wait and see; for should he act prematurely, Chantecler would find it hard to forgive him.

The anticipation was so dense it clung to one like a shroud. In the background a chorus of bees, then wasps, and a group of cicadas amplified the buzzing of the crowd with echoes of their own. The atmosphere was electric!

Madam Guinea Hen, dressed in the latest creation of the slanted Peacock, the current rage among the sophisticated, flitted among the guests, throwing a comment here, a praise there, and in general, elevating or demoting this one or that. Her gown of glitter and spangles, while drawing attention to her seemed to accentuate the rolls of fat that resulted from old age and the "good life." The tracks around her eyes were deep and could not conceal the hard brittleness behind them. So instead of highlighting her few good features, the gown emphasized all of the bad. However, since no one had the temerity to criticize her bad taste, she received compliments to her face and derision behind her back.

When the Magpie announced the first of

the fighting cocks, all attention quickly focused on him. The guests formed a semi-circle, vying with each other for the best positions to view the entrance of these celebrities. Madam Guinea Hen hurried to the front and took a position next to the Magpie.

"Cock Campine of Italy," said the Magpie in a loud, stentorian voice as he adjusted his stance.

As the Italian Cock made a deliberate and grand entrance, the crowd broke loose with admiration. He was big and stocky, and his muscles, which were well worked, bulged from his sides. He was dark and swarthy and emitted a pungent aroma that preceded him like a blast of trumpets.

"The Bearded Cock Of Varna," said the Magpie, louder.

"A typical Slav," commented the Peacock to Madam Guinea.

"Yes," you can see the Slav soul we have heard so much about," she exclaimed. "Charmed beyond words, charmed!"

"Cock Cruzero of Spain," the Magpie called out. As the lean, but firm cock entered, graceful and formal, he bowed to Madam Guinea Hen.

"Your egg, I presume, was laid in the hollow of a vibrating guitar," she said. "Delighted and honored to have you!"

"The Gold-penciled Hamburg Cock," proclaimed the Magpie.

He moved stiffly forward and gave a slight bow. His breast was striped with black and yellow and his cocked hat stood jauntily sideways.

"My party will be famous," Madam Guinea Hen bubbled, and addressing him directly, exclaimed, "Oh what a wonderful waistcoat. What can it be made of?"

117

"Of Zebra," jested the Raven.

"You don't say," she cried. "It will be the pride of my life!"

In the same succession, the black, cox-combed amazon from Africa was introduced, then the Bantam cock of France, a perfectly formed dwarf with a cunning intelligence. And upon his heels came, contrary to tradition, a very large Oriental cock, head half-shaved, eyes slanted, and a glint peering through sinisterly. Then came the Yankee cock, the Arabian cock, the Indian cock, the Belgian cock, the Irish cock, one more identifiable than the other.

The excitement had mounted with each introduction and the crowd had reached such a peak that superlatives were falling like raindrops, so that when the White Pile cock from England was finally introduced, a unified cheer was given.

Madam Guinea Hen stopped short at the sight of his docked comb. Recovering, she rushed up to him, and then turning to the crowd said, "He wears nothing on his head! He wears absolutely nothing on his head! How incredible! How fascinating it is!"

The Raven nudged the Cat and in a conspiratorial tone informed him, "He is the champion! He has vanquished all other cocks the world over. Can you see the razors attached to his feet that are concealed by the dust?"

Madam Guinea Hen scampered around like a mad harlequin, pointing out to everyone the extraordinary head gear, the plumes and helmets, the double, triple combs, everything about the cocks which was already obvious.

"She has taken leave of her wits," Patou said to the Scarecrow who had grown ever more intimidated with each new entry. He felt terribly disheartened and remorseful.

Suddenly, as if swept clean by a huge ocean wave, the chaos of sound diminished to a whisper as all eyes scanned the Magpie. For standing there in her resplendent gold coat was the incomparably beautiful and radiant Claudine. Although dismayed by Chantecler's insistence to attend, she had decided to brave the circumstance and face the crowd with as much equanimity as she could summon. In reverse proportion, the more she tried to control her apprehension, the more intensely she radiated. She appeared in the flow of her gold coat to be surround by a halo.

"The Golden Pheasant," said the Magpie, proudly. "Our esteemed and respected Guest of Honor!"

In a moment, she was completely engulfed with admiration and praise. Embarrassed, she looked back at Chantecler who was being ignored. She was pained and felt a deep hurt for him. However, he stood proud and still until he could no longer be ignored. Turning to the Magpie, he said loudly so everyone could hear,

"When you announce me, pray simply say, "The Cock!""

The Magpie looked Chantecler up and down disdainfully, then out to the crowd and said, "The Cock!"

Chantecler stepped from the threshold and addressed Madam Guinea Hen sarcastically. "I beg your pardon, Madam, for venturing to present myself in this plumage!"

"Don't let that distress you," she replied, equally sarcastic. "We excuse you, of course! You come in your business suit."

"No, Madam, my best," he replied. "I'm sorry if it combines merely the green of April

121

with the gold of October! I stand humble, for I am the Cock, just the Cock, without further ado!"

Claudine deftly moved to his side and as gently as she could she took him by the arm and said,

"Come, dearest, come away with me!"

"No," he said, "I must stay where destiny placed me. I am useful here."

The crowd started to murmur its disapproval and Patou arose and growled menacingly. Chantecler looked over in that direction and was surprised to see it was Patou.

"Hello, good friend. I see you've broken your pledge," he said.

"Friendship demands it," Patou replied. "The air here is polluted!"

The Magpie turned to the Peacock and in a voice that could be heard beyond the group he was talking to, said, "He is vexed because of the illustrious cocks whom I introduced!" Then turning to Chantecler directly, he asked ironically, "What, my dear sir, do you say to these resplendent gentlemen?"

The Raven jumped onto the Scarecrow's shoulder causing him to stumble. He hissed into his ears, "It is coming! It will soon be over!"

Chantecler turned to the Magpie and with a flourish that mounted into a cascade of sounds, said,

"I say, my dear sir, that these resplendent gentlemen are manufactured wares, the work of merchants with highly complex brains, who to fashion a ridiculous chicken have taken a wing from that one, a top knot from this. I say that in such cocks nothing remains of the true cock. I say that those befrizzled, beruffled, bedeviled cocks were never stroked by nature's maternal hand. I say that it's all aviculture, and aviculture is flap-doodle! I say they are nothing but a variety of a variety!"

As the White Pile came forward, the crowd murmured in anticipation. He was tall, lean, and every muscle bristled with enormous power. He was almost twice the size of Chantecler. In a cold, cutting voice, he said ominously.

"I protest!"

Chantecler's eyes gleamed, and taut with tension, he exclaimed, "At last!"

"It is time to climb the stairs," said the Raven joyously, jumping to a higher branch.

Claudine began to tremble. She looked at Chantecler imploringly and said, "You are never going to challenge that giant!"

"I am," he stated firmly. "To appear tall all one has to do is simply talk on stilts!" And turning to the White Pile he continued, disdainfully, "Let me tell you that you look like a fool who has mislaid his coxcomb!"

The White Pile was astounded by his audacity. In short, sharp blasts he said, "Fool! Coxcomb! What! What! What!" He moved in closer, indignation glowering from his eyes. "Do you know I have killed numberless cocks the world over. I am a champion!"

"And I, my dear sir, have never killed a thing! Not a fly, a flea—nothing! But I have at times succored, defended, protected, this one and that and I might, in my own fashion be called brave! You need not put on those mighty airs with me!"

Claudine ran to Patou and the Scarecrow pleading with them to intercede. As they moved to his defense, Chantecler warned,

"You keep out of this!"

Patou stopped, abashed, and taking a different tact said, "Go ahead! Go on and thrash him! The crowd is longing for the sight of blood!"

Chantecler looked around and saw the twisted anticipation on their faces. They could hardly contain their hunger for the blood letting. A sadness came over him as he said to Patou, "And I was never anything but kind!"

"Look at them and come to your senses," Patou pleaded.

"I say it's a disgrace," Claudine cried out in disgust. "A disgrace to the name of fowl!"

Chantecler raised his head and looked around again, disconsolate. And as he was about to withdraw, he realized he had gone too far, that he would be the laughing stock of the barnyard, his leadership impugned, so with a forlorn resolve, he said,

"So be it! The conflict is irrevocable!"

The crowd grew silent as the White Pile began to circle Chantecler. His tautly strung body formed a semi-curve, and with the sun reflecting from his bald head, he seemed like a crossbow ready to unleash its deadly arrow.

Chantecler maintained his nonchalance, but followed the eyes of the White Pile as he continued to circle. He caught a glimpse of the Scarecrow cowering and shouted out to him,

"Don't be frightened! Death is but the natural cycle completed! It is the style that is the true wisdom!"

The White Pile sprung quickly, delivering a vicious, downward blow. In a flash, Chantecler moved to his side and the blow fell with a thud to the ground. The impact was so severe, it raised the dust. The near miss broke the silence and raised a collective gasp of sheer awe.

The White Pile sprung back and re-formed himself. He began to circle when Chantecler feinted and planted a blow across his shoulders. The audience gasped as the

127

White Pile fell backwards. However, Chantecler did not follow up his advantage, so the White Pile put himself together outside of his range, aware now that his opponent was not going to be easy.

He again started round his path looking for the precise moment to strike. Chantecler waited patiently, on guard. The dallying annoyed the crowd which was thirsting for action.

"Where is the display?" shouted a disgruntled fan.

"The fireworks are a dud," shouted another.

"And he proclaims that the sun rises to hear him sing," a voice from the back of the crowd denigrated.

Chantecler was stung. He turned his head to the culprit and said angrily, "Yes, it is I who make the dawn appear!"

The White Pile, catching his movement, aimed a blow and hit his mark. The torn feathers flew wildly as Chantecler jumped back, sidestepping the rain of other vicious blows, until the White Pile withdrew and regained his posed position.

The impact had hurt badly, cutting him so that blood began to trickle from his shoulder. Chantecler sensed a heightened anticipation, but he remained cool.

"Thanks," he said lightly. "For the more I am mocked, insulted, flouted, and denied . . ."

The White Pile struck swiftly, but Chantecler was ready this time. He whacked him squarely on the head and a bruise rose quickly. Chantecler then finished his sentence, "Yes, the more I am denied, the stronger I grow!"

The White Pile was incensed with himself. He had been too cautious and Chantecler too bright. He would have to change his tactics. Without further hesitation, he hurled himself upon Chantecler with both feet forward. Chantecler was overwhelmed and tried to escape his grasp, but the White Pile held him tightly as he pecked away at his head.

Chantecler struggled frantically, surprised as well as severely wounded. Then with an enormous jerk he broke loose, tossing the White Pile backwards. He was bleeding around the eyes and was partially blinded by the blood.

The crowd was in a frenzy! They had responded to each blow with a vociferous confirmation of each spot that was accurately hit. Their frenzy distorted their faces and they looked grotesque.

Claudine was crying, beside herself with fear. The crowd, unaware of her presence now, had jostled her roughly. The Scarecrow had tried to shield her, but he too was thrown down. Patou placed himself between her and the crowd, keeping track of the fight as it developed. He was tempted to step in, but refrained, unsure of Chantecler's reaction.

The White Pile, sensing the kill, had attacked again, going in bluntly. Chantecler, aware of new tactics, parried him blow for blow, delivering a swipe here and there. The White Pile, stronger even than his great bulk indicated, kept pushing forward, aggressively. Chantecler felt his legs growing weak, and as the blood flowed past his eyes and from his other wounds, he knew his strength was ebbing.

The White Pile sensed Chantecler was on the wan. His vast experience confirmed the many signs of an imminent demise of an opponent. He increased the fury of his onset, driving hard, heavy blows everywhere he could.

The crowd was hysterical. They pushed and pulled each other to get a better view. Some were drooling from the mouth, and their eyes were aflame with a hellish fire. Claudine screamed, and sobbing called out to Chantecler,

"Stand up to him, darling! Hit him back! Please! Get up! Fight him!"

Chantecler, exhausted, bleeding, tottering, picked her voice out of the madness and digging as deep as he could, found a last reserve of strength, and with every remaining bit of energy, heaved for all he was worth. The explosion knocked the White Pile from him like a shot, but he raised himself and rebounded immediately. He quickly uncovered the two razors strapped to his feet and prepared to end it all promptly.

The crowd gasped audibly in horror, and before Patou could respond, the White Pile lunged for Chantecler lying on the ground exhausted. Instinctively, Chantecler rolled to his side in sheer desperation. The White Pile struck, missing him. He tried to stop his momentum forward, and to keep the sharp edges of the razors from striking a stone, he turned them inward. But unable to keep his balance he continued his progress forward, impaling himself on their points. Mortally wounded, he fell to the ground, dead!

Patou, Claudine, and the Scarecrow ran laughing and weeping and talking, all in one, to Chantecler who lay motionless, eyes closed, and utterly spent. Claudine cried out joyously,

"Chantecler! It is we! Speak to us! Speak, darling!"

As he opened his eyes and saw their loving faces, he felt a surge of new life. He had been spared! He had survived and he could bring the day once again! Tears fell from his eyes. Claudine took some straw from the Scarecrow and tufted a pillow under Chantecler's head.

A silence had fallen over the barnyard. The crowd had gathered as close to Chantecler as they thought safe, not knowing his response to their ugliness. Suddenly, a strange commotion agitated them. Looking to the sky, they scattered and ran for shelter. In a moment, pandemonium broke loose. Even the fighting cocks, including the fiercest, ran for cover. Some were quailing, others were petrified, and all were terror stricken. A dark shadow slowly swept over the bloodthirsty party-goers, who crouched and cowered everywhere.

"The Hawk," someone screamed. "The deadly Hawk! We are done for!"

Chantecler, bleeding, rose to his full stature and jumped onto the wheelbarrow. He called to Claudine to gather the chicks around him. They huddled, their heads drawn between their wings and pressed against him.

The Hawk was universally supreme! No one dared challenge his dominance. His swiftness was legendary, his strong clutching talons a bane, and the sheer power of his body cleared the field of any opponents making him sovereign. He struck terror everywhere he chose to go.

Claudine called out to Chantecler,

"He hovers over us! What can be done!"

The Hawk circled lower and lower, casting a deep, dark shadow that pervaded the barnyard. Chantecler braced himself and shouted toward the sky.

"I am here! Come to me! I will fight!"

The Hawk circled for the third time, then

135

coming in at an angle, swept past the chaos and inexplicably, flew away!

With this miracle of deliverance, the crowd rushed to Chantecler, overjoyed. They surrounded him, and in jubilation they were about to hoist him aloft.

"Stand back," he ordered. "I know your worth!"

They drew back hastily, trying to hide in the open.

"Come away to the woods with me," Claudine said, "Where the true hearted live! You shall be genuinely appreciated! It is my home and there is tranquillity there!"

The subdued crowd raised an angry murmur. Their instant hatred of her shot across the open space dividing them.

"You shall be silent," Chantecler commanded. "Evil does not reign here! It is she who has brought this place a grace and an enlightenment, never before fathomed so deeply. Her beauty is as the sun, brilliant and warm, a fountainhead of nourishment! Yet, as passionately, as completely as I love her, I will remain here!"

Claudine, dismayed, disappointed and crushed, asked him with total perplexity, "You will stay here even after finding them out?"

"Not for their sakes, dear one, but for the sake of my song," he replied. "It might spring forth less clear from any other soil. And now, to inform the Day that it is sure to be called tomorrow, I sing!"

The crowd obsequiously attempted to move in close once again.

Back! All of you," he exclaimed. "I have nothing left but my song!"

As they withdrew, Chantecler stiffened himself against the pain and started to sing.

His first notes were weak, and as he tried again, nothing would come. Desperately, he forced himself to concentrate. He saw the sound in his mind's eye, but only the scrawniest of whispers emerged. He looked crestfallen and pitiful. In excruciating despair, he cried out,

"I have nothing left! They have taken my song from me. What can I do? What else remains?"

Claudine embraced him tenderly, and as she caressed him, she said,

"Come away to the woods! In the tranquility of its peace you shall regain your song and your duty, ever reinforced, ever strong. Come with me, dear love!"

Chantecler grasped her tightly as a debt of gratitude overwhelmed him.

"I love you," he said, his eyes starting to

tear. And arm in arm, they left the barnyard and headed toward the forest.

A profound sadness filled Patou's heart. How he would miss his company and his friendship! Nothing would ever be the same again! He wished deeply for Chantecler to find his song and with it the happiness he so justly deserved. The thought raised his spirits momentarily, but the sadness over his loss overtook him.

The Scarecrow, too sad for words, grieved. He resolved that someday, somehow, he would find his courage and restore the inconsolable loss that hung like a pall over the barnyard. For now, he would try to raise Patou's spirts and hearten him.

X

❧

The Night
Animal's
Despair

As soon as dark had fallen, the Night Animals gathered together for their ritual. Their luminous eyes seemed to burn even brighter on this night. The Grand Duke, calling for order, started the chant that symbolized their unity.

"Chantecler must die," he intoned
"Chantecler must die," they repeated

And in succession,

"Chantecler will die!"
"Chantecler will die!"
"Long Live The Night!"
"Long Live the Night!"

When the incantation had ended, a low, grumbling murmur arose. The Grand Duke commanded, once again, the cry which made them all one. An owl, disgusted and discouraged, spoke up.

"Useless. It is all useless" he said.

"Useless?" exclaimed the Grand Duke, outraged. "What blasphemy is this!"

"They are just words we say," retorted the rebellious owl. "Shadow but no substance!"

And the Old Horned Owl confirmed the failure. "It is the truth. Our best plans have crumbled into ruin. Defeat has been our constant companion!"

"Yes—even the Hawk—he defied the Hawk! It's obscene," added the Barn Owl.

The Grand Duke accused them of spouting revolutionary ideas. Specifically, he described it as garbage. How dare they preach sedition! It would not be tolerated. Their discontent, however, was so strong they continued on.

"The Cock's actions are trumpeted in all corners," said the Barn Owl. "His notoriety is everywhere!"

The Grand Duke decided to change his approach to the uprising and tried countering with logic.

"They are mere words! His praise is temporary!"

"No! He is ruthless, dangerous," the Old Horned Owl said in outright insubordination. "He is indomitable!"

"We must give up," suggested a short, stubby bird perched on the third tier of branches.

The words "give up" traveled the rounds as if they were shot out of a cannon. The Grand Duke was shocked and indignant. True, they had tried many things that failed.

True, their opponent seemed uncanny in opposing them. But then again, Chantecler was no ordinary fowl! He was reinforced by pure virtue, and motivated by duty. His sense of destiny was difficult to corrupt, and corruption was the cornerstone of their lives! An underlying feeling that maybe the others were right slowly seeped into his heart. Just as he was about to concede to total defeat, the Raven, who had arrived late, jumped to the center of the group.

"Give up?" he shouted. "Did I hear you say we must give up! That we must quit, surrender?"

The owls looked at one another, then at the cat, who looked at the mole, who looked back to the owls, all asking if the question was directed to them, but by their action, implying it was directed to others.

The Raven repeated what he had heard,

but the babble of voices denied it. The Raven launched into a denigration of Chantecler, saying he was a fraud, for if he was so mighty, why did the sun fail to shine on certain days, or lay trembling on the horizon, desperately trying to ascend, but falling back into the darkness? It was because Supernatural Night was King!

The Raven had so sparked them that they repeated his phrase, "Supernatural Night is King!" they shouted. "Supernatural Night is King."

"Yes," confirmed the Raven. "He comes for you!"

Stimulated, encouraged and inspired, they chorused, "Yes! He comes for us! He comes for us!"

The Raven carried his sermon to an even higher pitch. He knew they were now with him and the thought fueled his intensity. He told them to be happy, that as birds of a feather they could overcome any enemy, no matter how strong!

Their exuberance became hysterical, reaching the edge of madness, and as the Raven completed a passage they punctuated it with "Supernatural Night is King! And alternated it with "He comes for us! He comes for us!"

And when the Raven described Chantecler roasted in a pot, cut up into bits and pieces for soup, as chicken salad, even pate, their exhilaration erupted into jubilation. They hoisted him to their shoulders exclaiming, "Supernatural Night is King! Supernatural Night is King!"

The Grand Duke was completely elated and grateful to the Raven for having saved his position of power. They were temporarily over the hump, he thought, but now, how to sustain? The Raven held out his hands for silence, then hopping down to the ground, he faced his admirers.

"Our celebration is premature," he warned. "Only with total victory can we savor full honor!"

A moan engulfed the gathering as the Grand Duke asked, "By what plan then?"

The Raven, his eyes burning with malevolence, said, "By reversing what was done! A broken body can mend in time. But break the spirit and he will turn in on himself, completing the destruction far beyond our measure! We shall break Chantecler's spirit!"

"But how?" asked the Grand Duke.

"By his enormous vanity," replied the Raven. "His one true weakness is women! Specifically, a woman, the proud, independent, gloriously beautiful Claudine!"

149

"And so?" inquired the Grand Duke, still not quite understanding.

"When vanities collide, my friend, betrayal prevails," said the Raven. "Through Claudine, we shall deceive Chantecler with the enchantment of the Nightingale who lives in the forest. And once time is suspended with the beauty of the Nightingale's sound, Chantecler will come to know that dawn arises without him!"

Again, the Raven was a sensation. Impressed by his cunning, his inventiveness, his fathomless evil, the Night Animals complimented him as brilliant, superb, and a true genius!

The Grand Duke, trying to suppress his strong feelings of apprehension, cautioned, "Beware, having failed before, we must not fail again!"

"We will not fail," the Raven assured

him. "You must trust me! You must believe! Supernatural Night is King! He comes for us!"

As if on cue, the inspired, grotesque band repeated,

"Supernatural Night is King!"
"Supernatural Night is King!"

The Grand Duke raised his arms, and in a deep, sepulchral moan, intoned,

"Chantecler will die!"

As in a trance, they joined the closing ritual.

"Chantecler will Die!"
"Chantecler must die!"
"Long Live The Night!"
"Long Live the Night!"

Then they all disbanded while it was still dark, in the spirit of camaraderie, confident that before long their torment would be ended and victory theirs.

XI

The Forest

The tranquillity of the forest was a soothing balm to Chantecler's wounds. In almost miraculous time he had healed his body, and with the tender, devoted and loving care he had received from Claudine, his song returned sufficiently so that he could do his duty.

His felicity was also due to the inhabitants of the forest, who had welcomed him with an abundant spirit. They possessed a gentleness, and as Claudine had stated, a civility that in its refinement created a grace which was conducive to amenity.

He liked the huge trees thick with gnarled roots. At the base of one of the trees, time or a stroke of lightning had hollowed a chamber. Stretched between two ferns was a great cobweb spangled with water drops. In the evening, when the spider web was touched by the moonbeam, it looked as if it were sifting silver dust. Even the height of day was a time of serene silence and coolness.

One morning soon after his battle, while still not completely recovered, he had made a strenuous effort to raise the sun. Although the results were a fine new dawn, he had become tired as he made his way home. He stopped to rest, and unknowingly, lay hidden from a gathering of forest animals. From their voices he could tell that the Rabbit, the Doe, the Hare, the Squirrel, and the Swan comprised the majority. He was at first going to join them, but their conversation arrested his movement.

"A new day—Chantecler has brought a new triumph," said the Rabbit. "Since he joined us, the forest is fresher, dewier, brighter—more alive!"

"Yes," added the Doe. "Broken and

bruised, he has mended here and in turn given an amazing grace to our greenery!"

The Hare spurted a few feet, stopped abruptly and said, "His spirit inspires my heart!"

The Squirrel dropped his nut and interjected, "That is true! I even feel the joy of swift motion more keenly!"

"And I, the thrill of fearlessness," said the Hare.

"And I, tears of happiness," said the Doe.

Then two voices from further back piped up. "And I, the softness of tranquillity," said one. "And the warmth of a great smile," added the other.

The Swan, sitting regally, but ineluctably burdened said, "And I, a love so strong it fills my heart to bursting. But I fear that Chantecler will exhaust his ever needful strength. The cost of his effort is monstrous!"

"But he has it to give," said the Squirrel, reassuringly. "He has a special reserve from which he digs, and it replenishes itself!"

"That may be the appearance," said the Swan, "But appearances are known to deceive!"

Chantecler felt a pang of guilt. Upon his arrival, Claudine had elicited a number of promises from him. Namely, that he was to restrict his singing to a few practices. In addition he had given the impression that he no longer thought of his barnyard. She had become very dominating, shielding him from the enthusiasm of the others, who desired his attention. He had begun to feel the restrictions keenly, but in his debt of gratitude to her, not wanting to displease, he simply resorted to performing away from her eyes. Concerned that the gossip would eventually get back to her, he decided to try and end it now.

"Who deceives?" he inquired, stepping into the center of the group. Chantecler looked directly at the Swan, who moved back shyly and lowered her head

"It is nothing," she replied, raising her head slightly. "Just chit chat among friends."

"Your shapely countenance says differently," he commented, gently.

The Squirrel rose on his hind feet and said brightly, "I think it is . . ."

"It is nothing, I say," said the Swan, cutting him off.

"Come now," admonished Chantecler, ever so gently. "Let us not be harsh. Let us have good cheer. I've brought a new day. We shall chase away doubt, anxiety, worry—all the things that chip away the joy of living!"

"I cannot," she said dolefully.

"Yes you can, my dear, if you try," he said encouragingly.

"I cannot," she repeated. "My heart aches for you! What if your source of strength should diminish?"

Chantecler was alarmed. The true meaning she was disguising, he realized, was that she loved him! He was flattered, of course, but recalling Claudine, he knew it would be intolerable to her. She had even come to the point of thinking the sun was competing with her! He would have to do something quick, he thought, to lead the Swan to another course.

"But it shan't," he said. "Don't you see? Your very concern is my strength. You love me as I love you, as we love each other. It is the act of loving that multiplies itself. That is my source. It forever replenishes!"

The Squirrel, the Doe, the Hare, and the others, ingenuously confirmed their approbation, and all in one said, "I love you!"

The Swan too, allowing the nobler aspects of his concept to prevail, joined in.

"Yes! We love you very much!"

"And I too love," Chantecler said, relieved. "I love even the smallest expression of the flower, the whisper of the wind, the inspiration of the sun, the very breath of life! I love life! I love everything in life! And now, let us go forward with good cheer!"

As they began to disperse, overflowing with enthusiasm, the Rabbit saw that Chantecler had stepped dangerously close to a trap.

"Beware the snare," he warned. "The hunter placed it there—hidden! He vowed he would capture Claudine! And that he would keep her on his farm, caged!"

"Ha! Ha!" Chantecler laughed. He flatters himself! Don't be frightened. She is not so easily dominated!"

161

"You know," continued the Rabbit, "that if you put your foot on the spring . . ."

"I know all about snares, my little man," Chantecler interrupted. "The thing shuts. It's a lesson for all! Now, to your duties—alertly, cheerfully, happily!"

They dispersed in various directions. Chantecler, however, remained, alone and deep in thought. I spoke glibly, he reflected. I spoke too easily of love. True, it gives strength and replenishment, but only with compromise. It brings a tranquillity, but after unrest and conflict. And it brings fulfillment, but only after frustration. It creates a purpose, but only with obstacles. In its singleness rests duplicity. It is the bitter with the sweet. It is a paradox!

And Claudine was such a mystery. He loved her. She was like Spring emerging from Winter's hibernation, bursting with the freshness and brilliance of the myriad colors of the flowers in bloom. She was warm and wise and able to see through his most subtle deceptions. And once she had revealed those deceptions, she would break his fall from grace and carry him to the sky in celestial arms.

The moment he thought he possessed her, she seemed to change into the unknown. The moment he thought they were one, she asserted her uniqueness and they remained two. He knew he would never understand her completely, but she brought him an indescribable joy. He tried visualizing life without her, but he couldn't. Love was a paradox, he concluded, and he had spoken of it like a fool!

The contemplation had tired him. He found a cool, shaded spot under an old and wise tree and closed his eyes hoping for a surcease from the many contradictions.

XII

The Evil Plan

The moment Chantecler departed the barnyard, gossip began to circulate, pointing its finger to the Raven. Anarchy had taken over. Everyone was doing precisely as they pleased. Consequently, disagreements arose leading to many fights. Not only had great tension developed, but the barnyard was cheerless as well.

Although Patou and the Scarecrow had emphatically confirmed the Raven's part in the proceedings, their accusation was discounted because it was well known that they were Chantecler's loyal friends. As the situation grew worse, however, some of the dissidents defected to their side, causing the Raven more and more ugly confrontations. With friction mounting steadily, the Raven decided to leave for a while, and put the second plan he had expressed to the Night Animals into operation. He devised an elaborate excuse that would account for his absence and set off to the forest.

On arriving, he searched out his allies: the toads, the frogs, the wolf, the spiders, the rodents, the snakes, all who crept and crawled. And while their mortal enemy was the Nightingale, whose beautiful song lifted ominousness from the night, they detested Chantecler as the Nightingale's sinister counterpart who had brought an even more powerful scourge to their home. The Raven explained his plan to them and enlisted their help and support. After they told him where he could find Claudine, he bid them good fortune and departed.

He made his way through the forest, confident that soon it would all be over. After searching here and there, he discovered Claudine dusting some extraordinarily beautiful, large and colorful flowers. They were exotic and rare and needed special tending to survive. The Raven thought she was even more beautiful in this setting, complimented by the flowers, than she had been back at the barnyard. His desire became inflamed and he vowed he would make her his own once this business was over. To appear casual, he maneuvered himself so that he would come upon her from the front. As he approached, he said lightly,

"Fancy meeting you! The world does diminish in size."

"Ah, what a surprise!" she exclaimed, startled. "How is it you are so far from home?"

"I am on an excursion," he replied, "To broaden my horizon! To expand my mind! To see the exoticism your forest offers! That your own golden beauty reflects!"

Claudine turned on him unexpectedly, and in a cold, precise manner, informed him, "My beauty does not reflect. My beauty is. I am its source!"

"Pardon me, Madam, do pardon me," he said, stalling for time as he tried to regain his balance. "One must know the intricacy of the maze to flatter simply. I only meant to say that you are beautiful!"

"I am beautiful," she replied to what she already knew was obvious.

"So you are," said the Raven realizing he had better change his tactics. "And how does the great Chantecler fare?"

A danger signal sounded immediately, and as if the floodgates had broken, the nightmare of Madam Guinea's came rushing back. She remembered the anguish, the terror, the unspeakableness of it all. And she remembered that it was he who had provoked

Chantecler into attending. He had always been insensitive and cruel from the beginning. She became wary and on guard.

"And why do you ask?" she said.

"Because we are old friends," he replied. "And he has always been a source of inspiration that bestowed scope and stature!"

She knew this to be a total untruth! His cunning and deceitfulness, his presumption to think her a fool, angered her.

"Let me tell you something, Raven," she said. "To grow, to gain in stature and scope, to be great like Chantecler whom you so admire, you must first divest yourself of your obliqueness, indirection, circuitousness and deviousness.

"Simply put, Madam, I am complex," he countered.

She ignored him and continued her assault. "In addition, you must also rid yourself of indecision, irresolution, oscillation, and fence sitting. You need to make a commitment!"

"I have said many times, and I repeat, Madam," he responded, "I am like the artist, I observe!"

"You tarnish, you pollute, you debase," she added savagely.

"I," said the Raven, stung to the core. "Remember, you are the one who holds pretension! Your golden beauty is but a copy of the male's. Your love of Chantecler—that he makes the sun rise—but an illusion!"

"How dare you!" she challenged. "It was your calumny, your false friendship, your distortions that led Chantecler to the Guinea Hen's and near to death!"

"I spoke fact," he shot back. "And in Chantecler's own words, To be forewarned is to be forearmed!"

"In all you say, in all you do, you have always been, will always be, second rate," she said with finality.

"And you Madam," he said burned, but still keeping his cool, "Will always remain second best!"

"Ha! Your second best coming from a second rate carries its own stamp," she laughed.

"No, Madam," he said, fully aware that she had fallen into his trap. "Facts are facts. They carry no one's stamp!"

He then rapidly launched into his assault. He pointed out how she was second to the sun in Chantecler's life. How his love was one-sided, to be used when he wanted, when he needed, when it suited him. But his duty to the sun was constant. He put his best into his song to woo *her*, but what she received was left-overs, a diminished, weak and definitely second best effort. And when he was away from his duty, he thought constantly for the morrow, and not of her. In her absence it was *she* he missed and not her. As his barrage mounted it grew more unrelenting and vicious. The truth of what he was saying finally struck home to her heart. And in torment, she cried out,

"Stop it! Your twisting and turning is destroying my love!"

"I," he continued pitilessly. "It is you, my dear, that is divided! I assemble, construct—I build a monument to your love!"

"With deceit, on false grounds?" she gasped.

"No," he said, for the final blow. "Realistically, with the truth!"

She was vanquished. She knew in her heart of hearts that he had been accurate. Although her golden plumage was every bit as beautiful as the sun, she was still second in his life. He loved the sun more!

The Raven, secure in his victory, now started his rebuilding process. He told her that although fate had brought the sickness, he had the cure. He reassured her that once they had executed his plan and destroyed Chantecler's obsession, she would reign as Queen of his Heart. He told her she was incomparably beautiful, that it was her unassailable right to reign and that it had to be! That it would be! She was but a step away!

"But how?" she asked, now intrigued.

"Simple," he said. "Silence Chantecler's song, remove his foolish notion that he brings the sun, and facing that fact, you will then be forever more, first!"

"But how can we silence his song?" she asked. "Your solution poses an insurmountable problem!"

175

"I'm surprised, Madam," he replied, "that your incomparable beauty left no room for the renowned beauty of the Nightingale's song!"

"What does the Nightingale have to do with me," she asked, puzzled. "What has he to do with the problem?"

The Raven explained that the Nightingale's song was so beautiful, so sonorous, so compelling, that once heard, it enchanted. And with the magic of enchantment, time flies, and with the passing of time, night passes, and with the passing of Night, Dawn will have arrived without Chantecler's song!

Claudine immediately grasped the genius of his plan. It was so simple she wondered why it had never occurred to her. The Nightingale was famous! She also remembered that one had to be in his presence for the enchantment to take effect, otherwise one only heard the echo of his song. An alarming thought intruded itself upon her.

"But it will be dangerous," she said. "Harm will come to Chantecler!"

"No," reassured the Raven. "It will only break his spirit. Our brethren, if you recall, tried to break the body. One can recapture the spirit at another time, but never the body!"

"You are right," she said ecstatically, and with a flush of gratitude. "But how can I ever repay you?"

By remembering me as special in my way, even though I am devious, distorted, and second rate," he chided, ironically.

"Hush," she said, repentant, "You are not! You did not deserve harsh words!

"Thank you kindly," he said. "But now, I must hasten back to the barnyard, where I am at home."

She asked him to stay a while longer, but

he refused, knowing that should Chantecler see him, his suspicions would be aroused, jeopardizing the plan.

"Success," said the Raven as he took leave. "Long Live the Queen!"

Claudine grew pensive and preoccupied. She was elated, but as she examined the situation further, her enthusiasm began to wane. Why should she have to do this? Wouldn't his love be diminished by this method? What would happen if she won the battle, yet lost him? And more disturbing, didn't the test of true love lay within her rather than him? She felt that if she loved him truly, he should be able to follow his vision. Didn't love engender greater concern for the beloved rather than the one loving? Had she placed unnatural burdens of faith and trust on him, tipping the scales unfairly in her favor? Was he there because he wished to be or because he had no choice?

Her thoughts drifted into fantasy. She visualized a time of living and loving in joyful harmony, in a land where all were free to do as their hearts commanded, without conflict and demand, without orders and payment, where everyone lived without danger or punishment, where life was idyllic and dreams were real.

But would this ever be possible, she asked, coming back to reality. The doubt hung heavy. All of a sudden she felt an intense need for Chantecler. She wanted his embrace, his caress. She wanted to be kissed and to feel the warmth of his smile. She wanted to be reassured. Trembling, she hurried off to find him.

XIII

The Lie

Chantecler's dream had taken a bad turn. He awoke and searched about for work to do. Though he had a semblance of routine, he was essentially at leisure, reinforced by Claudine, who did not want him to squander his energy. In addition, the pace of the forest was slower than that of the barnyard, and in its way had an organization all its own. So, by the time late afternoon arrived, his anxiety would reach an excruciating peak. In a moment of revelation, he realized his unrest was due to homesickness. He missed the barnyard!

He remembered that Patou and he had devised a way whereby, when at a distance, they could talk to one another. They had prearranged a signal, a vibration that traveled underground, that would occur at certain times. The sunflower was the instrument chosen, and when Chantecler was ready he was to hold the stem, concentrate fully, and the energy from his body would be transmitted, causing the sunflower next to Patou's kennel to vibrate.

He had decided to call, then changed his mind. He was off and on constantly, until late one afternoon, when he made a final determination that he would, although he knew that should Claudine find out, she would be most disappointed.

But his need was too strong. He found a sunflower and sat by it until it was the proper time. Then holding it tightly, he concentrated and felt the energy transferring itself. In a few moments he heard static and then Patou's low, mellow voice emerging. He was so excited, he was like a little boy again.

He could hardly contain himself as Patou related the goings-on of the barnyard. The fence had broken and the goose had strayed in, the youngsters were misbehaving, the hens were unruly, and although Madam Guinea had grown older, she was no wiser.

He told Patou how much he missed them. He asked if he had noticed the sun shining brighter, as that reflected his growing strength. He then reassured Patou that he would soon be well enough to return and that they would have fun once again.

Patou got to the serious business of the anarchy, the fighting and the unrest. He told how the Scarecrow was pining and had become the prey of vicious birds led by the Raven. But that the tide was beginning to turn against the Raven.

Chantecler was so engrossed in listening to Patou, he did not notice Claudine as she entered the area. She had, however, seen him and curious, withheld her greetings. As she quietly listened, she was upset to learn that he was homesick. She became angry at his delight in becoming a father for the one hundred and seventh time!

They are the ones for whom his heart beats, she thought. They are the ones who stimulate and excite him. And I can see that he and the sun have joined again as companions in joy. And he said he wasn't singing, but he was! He has betrayed me!

Chantecler turned and discovered her standing there. He knew in an instant that she had overheard his conversation. He was embarrassed and tried explaining as best he could, but in her anger, she would not accept it.

"So! So!" she shouted. "This clodhopper—this bird whom I picked off a haystack—I see that to rule his soul is apparently quite beyond my powers!"

Chantecler collected himself. He tried remaining calm, but a trace of resentment shone through.

"When one dwells in a soul, it is better, believe me, to meet the Dawn there, than with nothing," he said.

"No," she replied angrily. "The Dawn defrauds me of a great and undivided love!"

"There is no great love outside the shadow of a great dream," he replied. "How should there not flow more love from a soul whose very business it is to open wide every day?"

Claudine became hysterical. She stormed back and forth, her arms flailing.

"I will sweep everything aside with my golden russet wing," she said haughtily.

"And who are you," Chantecler said snidely, "Bent upon such tremendous sweeping?"

They stood rigid in front of each other, defiantly.

"I am the pheasant hen who has assumed the golden plumage of the arrogant male!" she said, her voice rising.

"Remaining in spite of all, a female whose eternal rival is the idea," retorted Chantecler.

Claudine demanded that he now deceive the Dawn for her sake, that he remain silent for one whole day. Chantecler refused saying that whatever lay in darkness too long became used to falsehood and consented to death. She probed him again trying to change his mind, but still he refused, adding that he couldn't stand to see the world plunged into darkness one moment more that was necessary. She was exasperated. Her frustration saddened him and he tried to remind her of other days.

"I shall never forget," he said, "there was

a morning once when we believed equally in my destiny, and in that radiant dawning love you forgot, and allowed me to forget, your gold for the gold of dawn!"

His reminder of dawn only infuriated her more. She determined, once and for all, to win. Impelled by her fury, she decided to follow the Raven's plan.

"Do you know what I think?" she said in a very controlled voice that belied her anger. "Shall I tell you the truth? You say you sing for the Dawn, but in reality you sing to be admired. You are a songster, nothing but a songster! You may not be aware of it, but your poor notes raise a smile right through the forest!"

Chantecler was well aware that she was trying to reach him through his pride, so he remained silent, hoping she would calm down. However, she continued at a higher pitch.

"I doubt if you can get as many as three toads and a couple of sassafras stalks to listen to you, particularly when the ardent Nightingale flings across the leafy gloom his melodious notes!"

Chantecler turned and walked away, hurt. Claudine followed him insistently.

"The echo must make some rather interesting mental reservations, one fancies, when he hears you sing after the great Nightingale. Have you ever heard him sing?"

Chantecler felt sick. She had descended to such a low state, he felt ashamed and responsible. Yet, he was infuriated with her constant comparison of him to the Nightingale. He turned to her and said,

"I have never heard him, and I have no desire!"

Claudine noticed four toads who were watching the fight with glee. They gave her a sign to indicate they were aware of the part they were to play. Resigned, she reluctantly returned the indication, and began to withdraw.

"I am exhausted with all of this bickering," she said, "I will retire."

The big toad called to Chantecler. He turned and was struck by the toad's utter ugliness. He and his three companions were so ugly they were repulsive! He was about to dismiss them when Claudine, detecting his repugnance, said,

"I hope you can be more civil to them than you were to me. They are friends of the forest and your reception will be broadcast. Good night!"

She withdrew into her roost, and from the small slit in her closed eyes she watched intently, eagerly anticipating the development.

The Big Toad, who was evidently the leader stepped forward and in a grand gesture said, "We welcome the great Chantecler whose song, at once novel, is lucid, succinct, pure and great!"

Chantecler, still smarting from Claudine's remarks, was flattered, and although still repulsed by their ugliness, felt more inclined to receive them.

"Pray be seated," he said.

"It is true, we are ugly," said the Big Toad.

"No! No! Chantecler denied, dissemblingly. "You have fine eyes!"

The toads ignored him and continued to flatter him by saying they had come to pay homage: that his song was celestial, terrestrial, a true song, and that by comparison, the song of the Nightingale sank into insignificance.

Chantecler's ears picked up at the men-tion of the Nightingale, and not quite sure of his hearing, asked, "The Nightingale's song?"

"It is not a circumstance to yours," declared the second toad.

"It is high time that a new singer came," added the third toad immediately. "And a new song, a song by a stranger who has come to change conditions here!"

"And you think that I shall change conditions?" Chantecler inquired, knowing full well their meaning.

The Big Toad puffed himself up and the others followed suit. He then croaked while still inflated.

"Your song has exposed the artificiality of his!" And then, as if on cue, the others exploded with, "Glory to the Cock!"

Chantecler accepted their flattery gladly. He was pleased to know, contrary to Claudine's contention, that the forest didn't think

193

so poorly of him after all. The Toads then overcame his last modicum of modesty by telling him he was extremely important, integral and indispensable. By this time, the toads even began to look attractive to him.

Claudine peering intently, saw that his head had been turned with the outrageous flattery. It would be only a moment longer before he fell completely, she thought.

The toads continued their diligent adulation. They had escalated it to the point where they were now singing the false praises. They told him it was he who made their hearts brave and uplifted their spirits so they could see beyond their lowly position to the great vistas of the world. And when they shouted that the sun would never shine so brightly without his song, he was ready to embrace them, warts and all. Their enthusiasm grew so raucous that they jumped and croaked and set up such a racket that Claudine came out onto the branch.

"What is all this noise?" she asked, irritated.

"It is the forest contingent," Chantecler said, elated. "They have shown me that it is all up with the Nightingale. He sings sentimental mush!"

"Ah! You are a songster! A fool!" she said cuttingly. "The Great Chantecler has stooped to an ugly, unjust judgement on hearsay. To please himself!"

Chantecler was stung to the core. He had never been unjust or petty! He went out of his way to elevate and praise. How dare she!

"You have maligned the Nightingale without even having listened to his song," she continued, taunting him.

Chantecler realized instantly the truth of her accusation. He was abashed and fully ashamed of himself for acting so, and said, "Yes, it is true! I have actually not heard his song!"

"This is most unworthy of you," she admonished.

The Big Toad bellowed stridently, "His song is superior! Should he but listen, he would judge for himself. His conclusion would only be stronger!" The other toads joined in, "Yes, it will be stronger!"

They all exited in a babble of chatter. Chantecler, reinforced by the certainty of the toads, eagerly joined, anticipating the joy of his forthcoming victory.

XIV

࿇

The
Enchantment

*A*s Claudine, Chantecler and the contingent of toads and frogs started out to search, night began to fall heavily, increasing the difficulty of locating the Nightingale. Claudine walked to the side of Chantecler, avoiding contact with his eyes for fear she would be betrayed. She was at once anxious for the end, yet reluctant for it to come. The toads kept up an incessant babble, constantly reassuring Chantecler of his triumph.

Suddenly, a sad and melancholy sound, heartbreaking in its fragileness, touched the soul of darkness. It was so tender, so poignant, so beautiful, it arrested everyone in their tracks.

The forest lay as if under a spell. The moonlight was softer, the tender green fire of the glow-worm blinked among the moss, the woodpecker nodded dreamily, and the rabbits with up-pricked ears, sat at their earthen doors, their moist muzzles pointed toward the source of music.

Chantecler raised his head to the sky, startled by the beauty of what he heard. "What is that?" he said, amazed.

"It is he," exclaimed the second toad.

"Yes," confirmed Claudine, "It is the Nightingale! It is the dear, sweet Nightingale!"

Chantecler knew instantly that he had been duped. What a fool he had been! What unbelievable stupidity it was to listen to their cant. How could he have been so unfair! Anger erupted from him like a volcano.

"Scum!" he said, "And you compared my rude singing with that divine sound! It carries a tenderness, a love. It is unsurpassed!

He started for the toads with a violence, trying to find their soft, flabby bodies.

"Disperse!" he heard the Big Toad order.

"That sweet, sentimental, sad song, sickens me!," stated another as he hopped out of reach.

"I am frothing at its syrupy confection," said the third toad, revulsed.

"Unbearable," said the last. "Disperse! We must welter in malignity!"

They were gone, quickly becoming one with the blackness of night. The dulcet strain of the Nightingale caressed Chantecler's ear once more, and turning to the source, he was irresistibly drawn to it.

"Sing, sweet bird, soar!" he shouted to the sky.

"Yes," Claudine repeated, "Now is the time! Sing! Sing! Sing!"

Chantecler reached the fountain of harmonious notes and stood transfixed beneath the tree. The Nightingale shone forth so crystal clear it was as if he, Chantecler, were the one singing.

The Nightingale's melody embraced him ardently. It was alluring, exquisite, graceful and captivating. Chantecler listened intently, enraptured. And then he began to make out the lyric. Its wisdom was so profound he could hardly believe it possible!

The Nightingale sang of forgotten roads of time that crossed the present making tracks pointing to the future. And at this intersection of knowing, endless and enduring, lay the fountain of joy and happiness. For it was the process itself that renewed fascination. It was intangible, yet not an illusion. It was a moment, yet for all time. It was now. It was ours to make beautiful, for Heaven was in our minds.

The more the Nightingale sang, the more bewitched Chantecler became, until the magic moment of enchantment possessed him.

In his vision he saw a beautiful world, a world of kindness, consideration, understanding and encouragement. Where help would be extended to one another with tenderness, and filled with grace. Where envy, greed, sloth and violence would be banished. Where pain, hurt, and poverty would have no place. Where everyone was precious. Where purpose guided, and love ruled. He saw a benign serenity, angelically soft and passionately inviting. He saw a world beyond anything he possibly could have imagined. It was so real, so immediate, so alluring, he extended his arms to touch it.

As the Nightingale sang, the time passed, and as the time passed, night diminished.

Claudine spread her golden arms to shield the light from Chantecler's eyes.

At the highest peak of the Nightingale's song, a thunderous shot rang out. The forest stood ominously still and silent.

Chantecler was jolted awake to reality to see the Nightingale fall wounded at his feet.

"The Nightingale is shot!" he cried out in anguish. "Oh my God! The Nightingale is shot!" He cradled him in his arms and began to rock back and forth. "Live, sweet Nightingale, so that I may live!" he despaired.

"I am deeply wounded," said the Nightingale in a whisper. "Alas, my voice is stilled. Dear, noble Chantecler, you must promise me to sing—always!"

"To sing?" Chantecler cried. "But how, after hearing the faultless crystal of your note? How can I ever be satisfied again with the crude, brazen blare of mine!"

"But you must," urged the Nightingale, pale and weak.

"How shall I ever find it possible to sing again! My song must always seem to me too brutal and red, " he responded, truly unable to understand.

"And I have sometimes thought mine too facile and too blue," countered the Nightingale.

"But how can you humble yourself to make such a confession to me?" he asked, upset.

The Nightingale gasped for air, and shuddered. "My friend," he said, "Can't you see the sorrowful and reassuring fact that no one, Cock of the Morning, nor the evening Nightingale has quite the song of his dreams?"

"Oh, to be a sound that soothes and

lulls," said Chantecler with a passionate desire.

"To be a splendid call to duty," replied the Nightingale, fervently.

"But I make nobody weep," Chantecler said regretfully.

"And I awaken nobody," he countered with his voice growing higher and even more lyrical. "What matters? One must sing on! Sing on, even while knowing that there are songs which he prefers to his own song. One must sing—sing until . . . !"

The Nightingale stopped breathing and lay still, a look of rest and peace upon his face. The anguish gripped Chantecler and tore from him a scream of pain that was heartrending.

"Nightingale! Oh, sweet Nightingale! He is gone! He is gone forever!"

He wrapped the Nightingale to his heart, tears streaming down his eyes. He was racked with an excruciating torment and an agony of sadness.

"Peace, my little poet," he cried sobbing. "You will be forever remembered! You will live here in my heart!"

XV

✿

The
Betrayal

Claudine, who was restlessly dividing her attention between the horizon and Chantecler, was deeply moved by his suffering. She was torn between wanting to console him and waiting for the sun to rise.

She moved tenderly to him, her arms outspread, still shielding the sun from his view. She could see that he was in deep shock. She put her arms around him gently.

"Come, my dear, come," she said. "Come and weep beneath my wing! You see how soft and comforting it is," she continued as he sobbed and lay his head upon her breast.

"Yes," he said in a smothered voice.

"You see that a wing is an outspread heart," she said softly. "That a wing is partly a shield, partly a cloak, and a place of rest. That a wing is a kiss which enfolds and covers you over."

She looked out over her shoulder and saw that the sun had risen to its full intensity and glory. Then, with a backward leap, she suddenly withdrew her wing.

"You see that the day can break perfectly well without you!" she shouted triumphantly.

Chantecler looked around, unbelieving. His head was whirling and everything looked blurred. He wiped the teardrops from his eyes, and surveying more clearly the incredible sight, the realization hit him like a mountain that had collapsed and fallen on him with a crash. An indescribable sound of utter agony convulsed him.

The mountain-top will be crowned in a moment!" she continued inexorably.

"No!" he shouted hysterically. "No! Not without me!"

"And now the horizon is gleamed with gold," she said, exalted.

Chantecler staggered and fell into a swoon. And as he lay exhausted and defeated, Claudine passed close to him.

"Can you see now that a heart pressing against your own is better than a sky which does not in the very least need you?" she said bitterly.

Chantecler was vanquished and completely helpless. He felt betrayed and utterly useless. The truth of her statement faced him down.

"And can you see that darkness, after all, may be as sweet as light if there are two close-clasped hearts in the shade?" she continued, unrelentingly.

"Yes," Chantecler agreed, "I see it all now!"

"And will I always be all in all?" she demanded. "Will I always be first—the Queen of your Heart!"

Chantecler nodded his assent.

"Then fling away your sadness and sorrow," she said, taking pity on him, "For even the Nightingale's purpose goes beyond his song. Know that he did not die in vain!"

"I don't understand," Chantecler said, confused.

"The sweet Nightingale was partnered with me," she explained. "He didn't know, of course, but together we have revealed that the Dawn would rise alone—without your song!"

Again, Chantecler fell back with a sob of anguish. He lay shocked and dumbfounded, the import still buried deep inside him. But like a clap of thunder, the true dimension of the horror overwhelmed him. It was impossible! She couldn't have done anything so base—so hellish! Slowly, the cognizance began to take hold. At first he pitied her, then an anger, so intense it frightened him, took possession of him.

"And for that he is dead!" he said furiously. So that you could reach the ultimate place in my soul!"

"Yes," she said staunchly.

"Treacherous! Selfish! Tragic!" he hurled out at her.

"And are you not selfish?" she fought back.

"But I loved you equally," he said, distraught.

"Well, I loved you more!" she countered.

"No," he exclaimed. "I pity you! We can never be together again! We must part! I will return to my farmyard—away from this sadness, trouble, and death!"

"They will know you no longer make the sun rise," she said, alarmed, but trying to maintain her composure. "They will know you are a fraud!"

"True, all too true!" he said, resolved that this was the end. "And yet I shall return. I have never run from the truth! I will accept that which is coming, which I have earned. In all, I am still Chantecler—greater than any ridicule that may be heaped upon me! Goodbye, you sad and pitiful creature!"

As he turned and walked away, Claudine's eyes followed him with a sorrow so profound it was unspeakable. As her eyes welled up with tears, she saw in a moment, a flash in the distance. She readjusted her sight and saw that the hunter had focused on Chantecler! He had seen him! She panicked as she saw the hunter break his gun in two and begin to load it. He was going to shoot Chantecler! In an instant, without thinking, she rushed toward the Hunter.

In a burst of passion exploding within her breast, she pleaded, "Dawn, touch the gun with your dewy wing! Trip the foot of the hunter in a tangle of grass. Let Chantecler live and I will dwell in the farmyard beside the ploughshare and the hoe. And renouncing for his sake all that in my pride I made a burden and torment to him. I will own, O Sun, that when you made his shadow you marked out my place in the world. Let him live! I abdicate! Oh Chantecler, how I love you!"

She saw the hunter's trap but a few feet away from her. Without hesitation, making great commotion to move the hunter to her, she ran to the snare and in an upward swing, she tripped the spring, which came down with a resounding crash. The reverberation caught the hunter's attention immediately.

Chantecler, hearing the sickening thud of the trap, looked back to see what innocent creature had been imprisoned. His heart sunk! As he ran to her he saw the hunter approaching. It dawned on him instantly what she had done! His soul filled with infinite remorse. She had saved him from death! She had become a prisoner, so that he might live! He was racked with an excruciating pain that tore him apart. He ran to the trap, and without a single word began tearing at it, trying desperately to free her.

"You must leave," she said horrified to see him. "The hunter approaches!"

"I will free you," he cried. "You cannot die! I will not let you!"

"Please, Chantecler! For my sake—save yourself!" she pleaded. "Go! The hunter comes closer!"

Chantecler worked frantically. He raised the trap slightly so she could remove one foot.

Claudine, hysterical with fear, saw the hunter within sight of the outer field.

"Please, Chantecler, you must flee," she sobbed. "If you love me as I love you, you must, for my sake, leave! I will somehow free myself and we will meet again! I promise you! But you must flee—or we are both lost!"

Chantecler saw the utter anguish in her eyes, and the pain in her heart, and with an abhorrent reluctance, he escaped the area, hiding behind a bush where he could view her.

The hunter arrived. His dog circled the trap, barking wildly. He sniffed furiously and in a moment had found Chantecler's scent. He bounded off in his direction, so Chantecler made haste to escape. Inexplicably, the hunter whistled the hound back. Chantecler continued to hover, desperate to see where they would take Claudine. Although the hound caught his scent now and then, his main purpose was to terrorize and secure Claudine. Chantecler tenaciously followed until he saw them come to the hunter's grounds where he saw them imprison Claudine in a cage.

Once the hunter had entered the chateau, and the hound his abode, where a hearty meal awaited him, Chantecler slowly and stealthily approached the cage. As Claudine turned and saw him, she almost fainted. Chantecler tried frantically, as quietly as he could, to unlatch the lock that held her cage closed, but it would not open.

Claudine whispered intensely, "Please, Chantecler, you must leave now—before you arouse the hound!"

Chantecler continued to try, his heart beating like a drum! Still the lock would not give.

Claudine frantically entreated Chantecler to escape, silent tears flowing in a rush.

"Please, my love, for my sake, show me the breath of your love and escape this horrible danger!"

Weary, and with a heavy and sorrowful heart, Chantecler conceded that he could not free her alone.

"Do not be frightened, my love, I will return with Patou and together we shall free you from this prison! No matter what the cost, no matter what the danger, no matter what the obstacle, I will return to free you, even though my life expires! I love you Claudine! You are first in my heart and you shall always be first!"

"And I will always be with you gladly, at your side, in whatever position nature deems, to help you bring the light and vanquish the evil of night." she vowed. "Run now! Escape so that we may meet again. Oh, how dearly I love you, Chantecler!"

221

As the hound dog growled and started to move about in his shed, Chantecler took one last sorrowful look at Claudine and started off on his journey to the farmyard.

XVI

A New Day!

*D*uring Chantecler's absence, the barnyard had come to see the Raven's insidiousness. They had traced their turmoil and unhappiness to his machinations. Eventually, they saw that his jests and the distortion of his words stemmed from an all consuming envy of Chantecler. And since an encounter with him left one in a state of depression, it wasn't long before they concluded he was the source.

Upon the Raven's return from the forest, confident that it was the end of Chantecler, he had become completely insolent and tyrannical. He had begun, in addition to the verbal lashings, to physically abuse the more defenseless.

In a moment of supreme arrogance, he related Chantecler's demise to the Cat. The Scarecrow, held in contempt by the Raven was allowed to overhear the conversation. He quickly ran to Patou and related the facts. Together, they returned and cornered him. While Patou snapped at his wings, the Scarecrow beat him with a broom, drawing the attention of the others. Finally, the Raven admitted his complicity, and once again tried to rationalize his way out of it. When that didn't work, he lightly poked fun at his actions.

However, this time, the animosity which had grown to enormous proportions, came down on him in force. The angry crowd built a prison in the center of the barnyard and confined him in it.

As Chantecler approached the barnyard, they had begun to grow mean. They poked and taunted the Raven without mercy.

Someone spotted Chantecler in the distance and shouted the discovery. They all hurried to the stone wall with great anticipation,

226

and vied with each other for better positions so they could see for themselves, his condition. They saw that he was weak and tired, and more importantly, that he seemed defeated, his shoulders sloped downward.

Chantecler saw them, but stoically walked through their ranks without a word. He went to the wheelbarrow and with great effort, he climbed it. He raised his hands and called for their attention. They quickly gathered round him to hear him speak.

"My friends," he said, faltering, "My friends . . . for just this last time . . . may I please have your attention. Since I left this home of happiness, warmth, and glory, I have come to suffer and know a deep sadness. A sweet, glorious Nightingale, whose song inspired tenderness, was sacrificed so that I might know the truth. And my Claudine, my beautiful pheasant hen of the golden coat,

227

who was my all in all, who loved me dearly and completely, who loved me to the end, became a decoy and is now imprisoned so that I may live!"

"Please Chantecler," said Patou, pained to see him brought to this pitiful state, "It is not necessary, my friend, to . . ."

"I must," said Chantecler, "For horribly, in my vanity, I deceived you! I debased the magnificent glow of the sun. I was dishonest, a fool, a fraud! I do not make the sun rise!"

The Raven, who had been listening with trepidation, saw his moment to become free. He called for their attention, whistling and stamping.

"I told you so!" he shouted from his cage. "He speaks the truth himself!"

Chantecler, seeing the Raven imprisoned, was surprised. "The Raven imprisoned?" he said, "And for what reason?"

The Raven shrieked, "For bringing forth the truth! For being virtuous! I, the Raven, virtuous!"

The Scarecrow and Patou rushed in closer. The Scarecrow, anxious to inform Chantecler accurately, said, "We have proved him evil! He is the one who has upset the balance and who nearly cost you your life, and us, much sorrow!"

Chantecler looked at his two friends sadly. "I am sure you have acted with courage and friendship," he said softly. "Your heart speaks volumes, but he is innocent and you must free him!"

The crowd was outraged and became surly. Chantecler jumped from the wheelbarrow and went to the prison and unlocked the gate.

"He is innocent," he repeated.

"The Raven is dishonest, he deceives,"

cried Patou, trying to make him understand. "I have discovered it was he, in cohort with the animals of the night, who had you to fight the gamecocks!"

"No, my dear friend, Patou," he replied softly. "It was my pride that led me there!"

"And it was the Raven who set Claudine astray with the toads," Patou continued, agitated.

"No, Patou," he replied. "It was my vanity that destroyed my lovely, beautiful Claudine. She showed me the truth!"

"So," said the Raven, snidely, "You are like every other ordinary Cock in the world!"

"No, Raven," he said humbly. "I am less. I am a fraud. I deceived. And for that I will never, ever sing again. I am muted forever!"

The crowd drew back in shock. It was inconceivable! It was impossible. How could

Chantecler not sing? What would become of them!

The white, fulsome Hen, filled with tenderness, said warmly, "But you inspired us. You gave us direction!"

"Falsely," corrected Chantecler. "It was the sun's rays pointing the way. I only grasped the rainbow!"

"But it was you that gave us purpose—to live happily, fully, to contribute gladly!" added the brown-speckled Hen.

"No," he said, "It was the sun, resplendent over all that illuminated the darkness, revealing the nature of each flower, each meaning, each smile—in just being! No, it was the sun that created the joy!"

The Scarecrow stood firm and tall as he said, "But you protected with courage!"

"Dear Scarecrow, with the sun as my

companion and ally," he replied, "I took false strength."

Patou, unable to restrain himself any longer, overflowing with love said, "You gave me friendship! You showed me loyalty, understanding, tolerance in my duplicity, and warmth! You gave me love! You must sing again!"

"No," he said sadly, "It is over, I am finished. My song is small, superfluous, unimportant. It has no meaning!"

"It is most important to me," pleaded Patou. "Please try!"

"But it would be a mere imitation," Chantecler insisted.

"No, my friend," he said impassioned. "While you may not live to see shining upon the steeples, that final light composed of stars clustered in unbroken mass, if you but sing faithfully and sonorously, and if after you, and long after that, in every farmyard its Cock sings faithfully, I truly believe there will never, ever, be night again!"

"Trash," said the Raven, spitting it out like dirt.

The Scarecrow jumped up and faced the Raven squarely and looking into his eyes said, "He is not! He may not make the sun rise for the world, but he does make it rise for me!" He was so forceful the Raven backed away, intimidated.

"What?" said Chantecler, surprised. "I make the sun rise for you?"

"And for me," said the white fulsome hen. "You cover me with warmth!"

"Is that true?," he said disbelieving. "Even with my confession?"

"Most true," said another. "For I love you!"

The brown-speckled hen concurred and said, "I love you!"

In moments, like the cascading of sparkling water, everyone was shouting,

"I LOVE YOU!"

Chantecler was taken with deep gratitude. His heart overflowed with happiness.

"My faithful hens! Patou! Scarecrow! How you make my heart sing with joy!"

"Then sing for us. Let sadness fly!" Patou urged.

"But can I? he wondered out loud.

They all gathered around him and said, "But you must!"

Chantecler cleared his throat and timorously made an attempt to sound his notes. It was weak and shaky. One of the hens imitated the sound of his morning call. Chantecler tried again and it came forth a bit stronger. Patou sang a register lower, giving support to the foundation. Again, Chantecler tried and a group of notes formed together into a phrase. Another hen joined, and then the others. Chantecler sang on top of their sound. He grew stronger and stronger, and caught up in his duty, he did not notice that each of the hens, then Patou, had dropped off. He was soaring once again on his own. He sang and he sang, the passion bursting from his breast.

And although it was already day, the sun hearing his amorous call, responded in kind and showered the barnyard with an illumination so brilliant, it covered the barnyard with a shimmering, golden coat. And rising from its reflection, one could see a huge form taking shape that resembled the Golden Pheasant. And if one listened closely, one could hear the words shouted loudly, "I love you!"

When the next morning came, the Scarecrow was once again in the field, hooked to

235

his post. He was so fearsome, no stray or predatory bird would even approach the field.

Chantecler put his arm around the shoulder of Patou and said, "Are you prepared for this dangerous mission?" my good friend. "I cannot free her golden beauty on my own."

"Together, we will free her—or die!" Patou vowed, as they set off to face the hunter and his hound.

In the distance could be heard the chug, chug of the ancient automobile. The farmer and his wife were returning. They were happy and cheerful, their loneliness having taken wing. Upon entering the barnyard, they were struck by the clean, fresh smell of the hay. Everything seemed to shine with a vitality they had never experienced before. A serenity and tranquillity had settled all around like a soft, gentle wind upon the wheat.

The farmer turned to his wife and said,

"It is nice to visit, but wonderful to be home!" They entered the house, grateful for the few simple pleasures they had, and so began another new day!

The End